W9-BIO-308

The morning after...

When Natalie had first begun working for Sam Erskine, he had tried to date her and she had turned him down cold. Sam had accepted that—Natalie was far too good at her job for him to risk seducing her.

But when Sam, a little worse for wear, proposed to Natalie at a party, she decided to play him along and pretend she believed that he meant it. The next morning, Sam had a giant headache; the last thing he wanted to be was engaged! Natalie wasn't herself, either. However, this dizzy, weak feeling she got whenever Sam was near was no hangover—she was lovestruck!

CHARLOTTE LAMB was born in London, England, in time for World War II, and spent most of the war moving from relative to relative to escape bombing. Educated at a convent, she married a journalist and now has five children. The family lives on the Isle of Man. Charlotte Lamb has written over a hundred books for Harlequin Presents.

Books by Charlotte Lamb

HARLEQUIN PRESENTS
1913—THE MARRIAGE WAR

Don't miss any of our special offers. Write to us at the following address for information on our newest releases.

Harlequin Reader Service
U.S.: 3010 Walden Ave., P.O. Box 1325, Buffalo, NY 14269
Canadian: P.O. Box 609, Fort Erie, Ont. L2A 5X3

Charlotte Lamb

Lovestruck

Harlequin Books

TORONTO • NEW YORK • LONDON
AMSTERDAM • PARIS • SYDNEY • HAMBURG
STOCKHOLM • ATHENS • TOKYO • MILAN
MADRID • WARSAW • BUDAPEST • AUCKLAND

If you purchased this book without a cover you should be aware
that this book is stolen property. It was reported as "unsold and
destroyed" to the publisher, and neither the author nor the
publisher has received any payment for this "stripped book."

ISBN 0-373-11935-6

LOVESTRUCK

First North American Publication 1998.

Copyright © 1997 by Charlotte Lamb.

All rights reserved. Except for use in any review, the reproduction or
utilization of this work in whole or in part in any form by any electronic,
mechanical or other means, now known or hereafter invented, including
xerography, photocopying and recording, or in any information storage
or retrieval system, is forbidden without the written permission of the
publisher, Harlequin Enterprises Limited, 225 Duncan Mill Road,
Don Mills, Ontario, Canada M3B 3K9.

All characters in this book have no existence outside the imagination of
the author and have no relation whatsoever to anyone bearing the same
name or names. They are not even distantly inspired by any individual
known or unknown to the author, and all incidents are pure invention.

This edition published by arrangement with Harlequin Books S.A.

® and TM are trademarks of the publisher. Trademarks indicated with
® are registered in the United States Patent and Trademark Office, the
Canadian Trade Marks Office and in other countries.

Printed in U.S.A.

CHAPTER ONE

NATALIE walked in through the swing doors to find the reception lobby already crowded. Waiting fans buzzed with interest, staring at her slender figure, smooth dark hair and quiet, restrained clothes before deciding she was nobody famous or important and taking no more notice of her. They were mostly hanging around to catch one of the radio station's biggest stars, Johnny Linklater, whose blown-up, grainy photograph stared down from the walls on either side of the reception desk.

A tall, rangy, carelessly graceful man in his mid-thirties, Johnny had a charm that hid a multitude of sins. His fans were oblivious of his flaws, of course; for them Johnny was perfect.

They should have seen him last night! thought Natalie, signing in for work. He had been incandescent, knee-deep in pretty girls, looking terrific in black leather jeans and matching knee-length boots, a scarlet silk shirt open at his tanned neck. Pure Hollywood. But all that glitter hadn't hidden from those who knew him really well a hectic desire to forget that the party celebrated his birthday, a day Johnny always dreaded.

Its arrival meant that another year had flashed past and he was one more year further on towards middle age. His birthday parties were acts of defiance. Behind his brilliant smile and light-hearted charm, Johnny was desperate, terrified of getting old, and although he could sometimes be irritating Natalie could forgive him a great deal for that secret vulnerability. It made him so much more human.

'Lovely morning out there, Susie,' Natalie said, exchanging smiles with the girl sitting behind the reception desk, a pretty blonde of about twenty, with round, saucer-like hazel eyes, who had only been working there for a few months and was still unable to believe her luck in getting the job. Natalie could remember how that felt. She, herself, had been over the moon at getting a job at the radio station when she'd started, but that had been three years ago; she was no longer starry-eyed these days—she had discovered that stars were just human beings under all the glitter.

Checking the time Natalie had written beside her name, Susie looked at her watch, then said, in disbelief, 'You're late!'

'So I am,' Natalie said cheerfully, amused by Susie's incredulity. Okay, she was normally one of the first to arrive, but why shouldn't she be late once in a blue moon? Nobody was perfect.

Adding two and two and reaching the obvious conclusion, Susie enviously asked, 'Good party last night?'

Natalie's blue eyes gleamed with reminiscence. 'I had a lot of fun, thank you.'

'Who with? Not Johnny?' Susie at once asked, eyes brimming with curiosity, but Natalie was not being drawn.

Laughing, she walked off to the lifts, knowing that Susie would soon hear about it; the news would be all round the radio station in an hour or two. Gossip spread like wildfire here, and a lot of the staff had been at Johnny Linklater's party last night. He had invited everyone who worked on his show, from the production staff to the girls in the programme office, as well as all the executives, including the head of the station, Sam Erskine, and Natalie, who was Sam's secretary.

Once the others got to work this morning they would talk of nothing else, but Natalie had no intention of joining in. Discretion was an important part of her job; she knew a lot of secrets and never let a single one slip. She would never have held down her job so long otherwise.

Her office was on the top floor with a view across the town to the sea. A hush hung over the entire corridor this morning, although normally phones were ringing and voices arguing from one end to the other. Most people on this executive floor had been at the party and would still be struggling in to work.

As she'd expected there was no sign of her boss yet, although Sam Erskine was usually there when she arrived each morning; he seemed to come to work at crack of dawn. He worked a twelve-hour day five days a week, and often on Saturdays, too, and he expected his secretary to work almost as hard—to get there early and go home late, like himself. This morning, though, she had been certain he would be late. He must have the hangover of the century, and serve him right.

Natalie began her usual morning routine at once: switched on her word processor, collected the mail from the in-tray, where it had been delivered by the boy from the mail room, and began opening letters, reading through them, sorting them into various piles in order of importance and urgency. The telephone began to ring a few minutes later and the fax machine chattered away from time to time.

The calls were all for her boss, of course; she scribbled messages on her pad, answered questions, fielded enquiries deftly without admitting that Sam wasn't yet at work. He expected the utmost discretion from her and she knew he would not want anyone to know he was in late that morning.

At a quarter past ten Natalie got a call from a friend in the advertising department who hadn't been at the party last night. Gaynor's voice was breathless with excitement.

'Is it true?'

'Is what true?' hedged Natalie, although she knew exactly what Gaynor was talking about and couldn't help smiling. But as Gaynor couldn't see her that didn't matter.

'Oh, come off it, Nat, you know what I'm talking about...the party last night? I just saw Johnny's producer, and she told me Sam had...'

Natalie heard a sound outside her office and hurriedly said, 'Sorry, Gaynor, somebody coming in...can't talk now, see you later.'

She hung up, but it wasn't Sam, it was only one of the producers, who hurried in asking urgently, 'Where's Sam?'

'He isn't around at the moment, Red,' fenced Natalie.

'Hangover?' She should have remembered that James Moor had been at the party last night. He was not much taller than she was, a cheerful, energy-burning man in his early thirties, with eyes the colour of chestnuts and a shock of bright red hair, hence his nickname.

She shrugged, not answering.

'Poor Sam. I wonder how much he remembers?' Red said, grinning at her. 'Well, get him to give me a buzz, will you, when he does show?'

He had no sooner gone than the phone began to ring again. Natalie glanced at her watch. It was half-past ten now, but Sam still hadn't shown up. Was he coming in to work at all today? Or was he hiding under his duvet wondering how to get himself out of trouble?

'Mr Erskine's office,' Natalie said, picking up the receiver, and heard a high-pitched female voice she instantly recognised.

'I want to talk to him!' it shrilled.

I bet you do, thought Natalie, but said in a blank, polite voice, 'I'm sorry, he isn't in the office at the moment. Can I take a message?'

Furiously, the voice shrieked, 'You mean he doesn't want to talk to me!'

'Who shall I tell him called?' Natalie said in her creamiest tone, smiling to herself as she pictured the other woman's expression. Helen West was a singer, a vibrant redhead, whose career had never quite got anywhere but who always behaved as if she were a big star. She had a temper as hot as her hair.

'You know damned well who it is!' Helen West yelled. 'And you can tell him from me he isn't getting out of it by hiding behind you. He's going to regret doing this to me! And so are you—don't worry!'

The phone slammed down and Natalie winced. Replacing the receiver, she looked at the clock. Twenty to eleven—where was he? Probably Helen West was right and Sam was hiding. From both of them. As well he might!

But he had a couple of really important appointments—he would have to show up sooner or later. Unless he had fled the country? No, he wouldn't do that. He would be here sooner or later.

She couldn't wait.

On going to bed the night before, Sam Erskine had automatically set his alarm for seven o'clock, as usual, but had slept through the peremptory ringing, which had finally died away leaving him to sleep on and on. It was well after ten when he finally stirred and turned over, yawning.

Opening one eye, he hurriedly shut it again as light blazed into it. 'Ohhhh...' he groaned, putting a hand to his thudding head.

After a moment he cautiously opened his eye again and looked at the clock, letting out a grunt of disbelief—what on earth was he doing, still in bed at this hour? It wasn't Sunday, was it? Warily he opened his other eye and sat up, groaning again as the movement increased the thudding in his head; he felt as if someone was beating a gong inside his scalp, sending shock waves through the rest of him.

Vague memories of the night before slowly began to come back. Of course. The party. Johnny's party. It must have been quite a night. Thank heavens Johnny only had a birthday once a year; too many parties like that could be life-destroying.

Pushing back the bedclothes, Sam swung his long legs out of bed and stood up, a hand over his dazzled eyes. Why was the sunlight so bright this morning? Why couldn't it have been one of those dark and rainy days, when the sky was like old grey flannel and there was barely enough light to see by?

Naked, he walked across the room to the bathroom. Sam never wore pyjamas; he preferred to sleep naked, especially in summer. It saved on washing. He paid a cleaner to come in once a week to clean his flat but she did not do his washing; Sam had to do it himself.

He had a routine of stuffing his dirty clothes into the washing machine every Saturday and ironing them on Sunday afternoons while he listened to rival radio stations and got ideas from any programmes he enjoyed, or made derisive notes on what he considered their failures. He quite enjoyed the hours he spent that way; he had come to like ironing, it was a soothingly boring occupation, kept his hands busy and left his mind available for a free-flow of ideas. Some of his best projects had come out of an afternoon ironing.

After turning on the shower he looked at himself in the bathroom mirror and saw uneasiness in his grey eyes, but couldn't think why it should be there. What was preying on his subconscious? He knew something was— if only he could remember what!

He hadn't crashed his car, had he? Hit someone? He stepped under the shower and gave a yelp of shock as his warm flesh came into contact with the cool jets of water.

At least this should wake him up! He showered rapidly, checking himself as he did—but there were no marks on his strong, angular face or the lean, muscular body below it. If there had been a fight he had not been injured in any way.

Maybe it was the other guy who had come off badly? he thought, grinning, not displeased with that idea. He hoped it hadn't been Johnny—the last thing he needed was a feud with his top star. But Johnny wasn't the fighting type. He was too afraid of damage to his face.

Something had happened, though. He just knew it. Ever since he woke up something had been hovering at the back of his mind, just out of sight, never going away but never letting him see it clearly.

What on earth was it?

As he towelled himself, and dressed in a red-striped shirt and dark grey suit, he chased the memory. Something had definitely happened last night and Sam couldn't shake off a growing uneasiness. Knotting his dark red silk tie, he stared into the dressing table mirror, not seeing himself at all, calling up memories of the party.

He had taken a taxi, which had stopped to pick up Helen who had been wearing pleated black satin which left a lot of her visible—bare white shoulders, half her high, creamy breasts, all her arms and even some of her thighs, glimpsed through slits in the long skirt.

She had looked sensational, and when Johnny had met them at his front door, he had gazed, open-mouthed. 'Wow, you sexy thing!' he'd breathed, arms flung wide. 'Give me a kiss!'

Johnny had been lit up, the life and soul of the party, as always, loving being the centre of attention, and Helen hadn't exactly struggled to escape his clutches.

She had been in one of her moods last night. All the way to the party she had been coaxing and badgering Sam on the usual subject. They had been arguing about it for weeks. Helen wanted to get married. Sam didn't.

He had good reasons for not wanting to get married. He had explained them all over again, he had been patience itself—but Helen had refused to accept them. In fact, she'd refused to listen at all. By the time they'd got to the party she'd been in a sulky, glowering mood.

She had given him a defiant look as she'd put both arms round Johnny's neck and deliberately leaned her sexy little body against him.

She hoped to make him jealous, he'd realised, watching her wryly. Well, she wasn't going to win at that game, he remembered thinking. He wasn't the jealous type. If she wanted to flirt with Johnny, let her. So he had wandered off to get a drink from the bar, leaving them together. Let them get on with it!

Bad move! he thought now, running a brush over his thick black hair. He shouldn't have started drinking so early. He rarely drank much; it slowed the responses, made thinking difficult, and Sam needed his brain in good working order all the time. His job required it; you couldn't run a radio station part-time—you had to be on the ball twenty-four hours a day because you never knew when a problem might come up. It was different for the broadcasters themselves; when they had finished their show they came off air and could go home and do as they pleased—they worked a fixed number of hours a day. Lucky old them.

If he hadn't started drinking as soon as he'd arrived he wouldn't have this headache now!

As he put his hairbrush down on the dressing table he stopped, staring at his hand fixedly. His signet ring was missing.

His heart thudded in shock. He almost never took it off. But maybe he had taken it off in the shower? He didn't remember doing it—why should he have done? But he hurried back to the bathroom and looked everywhere. No sign of the ring there.

Returning to his bedroom, he searched that, growing increasingly worried, but he didn't find the ring anywhere. He had worn it to the party, hadn't he? He must have done. He never took it off. It was very old and immensely valuable. Of massive gold, it bore his family crest. Sam was very proud of it and had worn it day and night since he first inherited it.

The Erskines were an old family from the Strathclyde area of Scotland; their surname was believed to be the Celtic word for a green hill and their crest represented that.

The shield it bore was divided into four, with the sym-

bol for a green hill in two opposing sections while the
other two carried a broken sword, no doubt because they
had been a war-like collection, his ancestors, always
fighting, although why the sword in their shield was broken Sam had no idea.

The ring had been in Sam's family for generations. It
was always given to the eldest son on his twenty-first
birthday, but in Sam's case his father had been dead by
then and the ring had been kept locked in a bank vault
for some years. The ring had been handed over during
Sam's birthday party, by his mother. Sam could remember the weight of it as it first slid onto his finger; it had
been far too big, and he had had to have it altered to fit,
but he had felt far more than the weight of the ring that
evening.

His mother had wept. 'His finger was much bigger
than yours.' She still mourned his father, who had been
a massive man, six feet six and broad of shoulders, deep
of chest, with large, powerful hands. Sam had been
scared of him but had loved him very much; he still
missed his father, too.

Jack Erskine had died in the Himalayas during a
British climbing expedition; the weather had turned
against them overnight, arctic conditions had driven
them back down the mountain and in a blizzard Jack had
missed his footing and fallen to his death.

Sam had been sixteen, too old to cry; if he had cried
he might not have taken the shock so hard. The bruise
of it was still buried deep inside his mind. Putting on
his father's ring had been a terrifying experience.

He had felt the weight of his entire family as he'd put
on the ring—aware of his mother, watching him with
pride and sadness, aware of his two younger sisters,
Jeanie, who was ten, and eight-year-old Marie, all of

them now his responsibility, which he knew already wasn't going to be an easy one. He had been aware, too, of the other Erskine eyes watching him. Dozens of relatives had been at his twenty-first party—and beyond them Sam had felt the centuries of family history stretching back to the fifteenth century, when their branch of the Erskines had first appeared.

He felt their shadowy presence now and shivered. If he had lost the ring, his mother, the family, would never forgive him—he would never forgive himself. It was priceless and irreplaceable. His finger felt bare without it.

He must have lost it at Johnny's party—but how? Maybe Johnny had found it by now. Sam walked over to the phone, which was still switched onto the answering machine. He flicked the switch to play back any calls and Helen's voice shrieked.

'I hate you. Do you hear? I'll never forgive you. Never.'

The machine clicked off. Sam put a hand to his head, flinching. There was a whirring noise and Helen's voice shrieked again.

'I suppose you thought that was really clever, didn't you? You did it to make me look stupid. Well, you're going to look pretty stupid when I've finished with you. I'm going to make you wish you were dead.'

Sam already wished he was dead. His head was hammering and his mouth was as dry as a desert.

Another whirr, then Helen's voice began again. Sam couldn't stand any more; he switched the recording off and hurriedly dialled Johnny's number, but got no reply. Johnny was probably fast asleep and would be for most of the day. Heaven only knew what time he had got to sleep last night.

Sam decided to try again later. Without bothering to have any breakfast, he left his top-floor flat in an apartment block on the promenade, with its breathtaking view of the coast, took the lift down to the underground car park, climbed into his little red MG, which he loved passionately, and drove off to work.

He needed some black coffee before he could think clearly; he would get Natalie to make him some when he got to the office. A frown pulled his black brows together. Natalie. Now why had her name given him another stab of uneasiness?

What had happened last night?

Fishing dark glasses out of his glove compartment, he drove along the promenade and up the short hill on which the radio station sat. The drive only took a few minutes. Sam often walked it, but today he wasn't up to the walk. Parking behind the building, he walked in through Reception, past the hovering mob of Johnny's fans.

The girl behind the desk gave him a lopsided, excited grin as soon as he came through the doors. 'Good morning, Mr Erskine! How are you this morning?'

Why was she smiling like that? Sam gave her a curt nod. 'Fine, thanks.' Stupid girl—what was so funny? That he was late for once? That he was wearing dark glasses? Okay, he had a hangover. So what?

'Cong...' she began, but he was already out of earshot, striding to the lift, passing a couple of secretaries who were chattering to each other on their way through the lobby. As they saw Sam they stopped talking quickly, only to begin giggling.

'Good morning, Mr Erskine,' they chanted as he strode past, and he got two more of those knowing, grinning looks.

He was glad to get into the lift and have the doors close on them all. When he got to his office he must ring Johnny first, and if there was no reply send someone over to wake him up, put him under a shower, sober him up and get him here in time for his show at noon. Dead or alive, Johnny had to do his show.

Sam walked into his office and found Natalie just placing a pile of opened letters on his desk.

She looked round, her sleek dark hair falling against her cheek, her blue eyes faintly amused, which irritated him. This morning Natalie was as cool and elegant and together as ever. No hangover for Natalie, who only drank orange juice or mineral water, or a single glass of white wine, or champagne on very special occasions.

'No morning after the night before for you, I suppose?' Sam muttered. 'You're too perfect to live.' It annoyed him just to look at her; she wasn't human—had she no ordinary weaknesses? He wished she had his head this morning. She should have agony stabbing away inside her temples.

She merely smiled. 'Would you like some coffee?'

'Black,' he said. He caught the sideways lift of her brows and added, 'Please,' knowing what that silent glance meant.

They had been working together for a long time. She knew him very well. Too well, he thought, glowering. What was she looking at him like that for?

Natalie went out and Sam absently watched her go. She was a slender girl, who wore much the same outfit every day: a white shirt, with small, pearly buttons, tucked into a smooth-fitting skirt—a black one today— discreet, demure, the hem just around the knee. She was only five feet four or so—a good eight inches shorter than Sam. Her legs were worth looking at—he looked

at them until she vanished. There was something about
the way she moved that had always got his attention.
Beautifully shaped ankles, too. There wasn't much of
her, but what there was Sam found very pleasurable to
look at. Pity she was one of the touch-me-not brigade.
He had never yet managed to get her closer than a foot
or so away, let alone into his bed.

Sam sat down behind his desk to check on the pile of
telephone messages, the neat pile of faxes. He read
quickly, absorbing them all, and had finished by the time
Natalie came back with the black coffee. She hadn't
reached his desk when the door crashed open and Helen
erupted into the room, her red hair windblown, her green
eyes flashing.

'Oh, so you are here! I knew she was lying!' she
yelled, then glared at Natalie. 'I knew you were lying!
You've never fooled me. I knew what you were after all
along, with your sweet pussycat smiles and your demure
office kit—the perfect secretary, ha ha. The minute I set
eyes on you I knew the sort of operator you are!'

Natalie took no notice of her at all. She quietly moved
to put Sam's cup of coffee on his desk, but Helen tried
to charge past her and knocked the cup flying, splashing
everything within reach with scalding black coffee.

Some of it went over Sam, some of it over Natalie;
Helen got splashed herself and that seemed to send her
into a positive frenzy.

'Now look what you've done!' she screamed at
Natalie.

'Are you out of your mind, Helen?' Sam angrily asked
her, looking at his coffee-stained shirt. 'You've soaked
us all! And don't try to shift the blame to Natalie…'

'Oh, no, of course not. She's just a sweet innocent,

isn't she?' Helen snapped, sarcasm loading every syllable.

'What on earth is the matter with you?' Sam wished
he could remember more about last night; what could he
have done to her to put her in this mood? Helen had
always had a hot temper, but he had never seen her like
this before. Her vibrant red hair seemed to be blazing
with rage, and her green eyes were cat-like with venom.

'As if you didn't know! You needn't think I care—I
only came to tell you I hate you and if I never see you
again it will be too soon for me!'

Her voice had gone up with every other word until
the decibels were loud enough to wake the dead—or at
least those of the radio station staff who had been to
Johnny's party too and were barely able to keep their
eyes open this morning.

Beyond this office the corridors and rooms were totally silent. No doubt everyone within earshot was listening with fascination.

'For heaven's sake, Helen, calm down! Surely we can
talk this out in a civilised manner,' Sam said in what he
tried to make a placating tone, but that only seemed to
make matters worse.

'Don't talk to me as if I was half-witted! You humiliated me last night, but that was what you intended to
do, wasn't it? Well, you aren't getting away with it.'
Helen slapped him hard across the face, gave a loud,
angry sob, then turned and ran out of the office, slamming the door behind her so that every pane of glass in
the room rattled and shook.

Sam swore, gingerly feeling his hot, stinging cheek.
'I'll swear she loosened some of my teeth! Remind me
never to get involved with singers again, will you? I

know musicians are always temperamental, but Helen takes it to ridiculous extremes.'

Natalie had mopped herself dry with a handful of paper tissues; she offered him the box.

'Dry yourself off. I'll get a clean shirt out for you.' He always kept a couple of shirts in the office in case of emergencies.

'Get me that coffee first,' Sam said, busily dabbing at himself with paper tissue. 'I need it even more now. My headache is ten times worse after listening to Helen yelling blue murder.'

'I'll get you some aspirin,' Natalie promised, going out. She returned a moment later with a glass of water, a couple of aspirin and a fresh cup of black coffee.

Sam looked at her gratefully; she never shouted at him or chucked things. She made his office life a haven of peace and quiet. 'What would I do without you?'

She gave him that curling little smile of hers, putting the coffee on his desk and handing him the pills and the glass of water.

'Oh, there would be some other woman around to wait on you hand and foot, no doubt.'

Ignoring the faint touch of sarcasm in her quiet voice, Sam swallowed the pills and a gulp of water, then handed her back the glass.

'Can you get me that clean shirt now?' He met her eyes again and added drily, 'Please, Natalie?'

'Of course, Mr Erskine.' She walked away to the cabinet where she kept his shirts, spare underwear and a pair of boots he sometimes used for outside broadcasts. Sam admired her legs again; they really were something. He'd like to see all of them one day, not to mention the rest of her. What did she look like out of her neat, demure little office outfits? Interesting idea, he thought, absently unbuttoning his coffee-stained shirt and taking it off.

Natalie came back with his clean shirt, glanced at his bare, hair-roughened chest then quickly looked away. Sam's mouth twisted. Hadn't she ever seen a guy naked? The idea struck him forcibly—maybe she hadn't?

What, a virgin, in this day and age? he thought, almost laughing at the notion. Not a chance. Rarer than unicorns.

He took the shirt she held out to him and slid his arms into it, began to fumble with the small buttons which ran down the front. They were so stiff he couldn't force them into place, and he impatiently abandoned the attempt.

'Could you do these damn things up for me, Natalie?' he muttered.

He could tell from the pause that followed that she was reluctant to do it—in fact, for a moment he thought she was going to refuse—but in the end she did come closer, and put out her hand to start buttoning.

He saw a glint of gold on one finger and gave a sharp exclamation, grabbing her wrist.

'You've found my ring! What a relief! When I woke up this morning and realised I wasn't wearing it I went into a terrible panic. My mother would kill me if I ever lost it. I searched my flat for half an hour this morning, and then I realised I must have left it somewhere at Johnny's place—I tried to ring Johnny, but of course there was no reply. He's probably dead to the world.'

'Probably,' she echoed, not meeting his eyes.

'I can't thank you enough for taking care of it for me,' Sam said. 'Where did you find it?'

'I didn't find it,' she said limpidly. 'You gave it to me.'

Startled, he queried her. 'Gave it to you?'

'Last night.' She nodded. 'At the party.'

'Did I? I must have been very drunk; I don't remember a thing about it.' His hand was still extended, but Natalie made no move to give the ring to him, and Sam's eyes grew wary. 'Can I have it, please? It's a family heirloom, you know, and very valuable.'

Surely to heaven she wasn't intending to keep it? No, of course she wouldn't—Natalie wasn't the type to do something like that. That would be tantamount to stealing. Okay, he might have given it to her, on some crazy impulse last night, but she must have realised he hadn't known what he was doing.

'You can have it when you give me the other one,' she said. 'Drink your coffee while it's hot; it will help you wake up.'

'What other one?' He was bewildered; what was she talking about? He must be slow on the uptake this morning. He picked up the cup of coffee and took a sip too fast. The hot liquid burnt his tongue.

'You said it would be a sapphire, to match my eyes,' Natalie said, with a gleam of happy reminiscence in the big blue eyes watching him.

'Sapphire...' repeated Sam, his stomach sinking as it dawned on him that she was wearing his signet ring on her left hand. On her engagement finger.

'You remember, last night?' Natalie said in a honeyed tone. 'At the party? When you proposed to me? In front of everyone?'

'Proposed...' Sam hoarsely repeated, going pale.

She gave him a dewy look. 'Yes. You went down on your knees, in front of them all...'

'On my...' he breathed, with incredulity and horror.

'Knees.' She nodded. 'And asked me to marry you.

You put your signet ring on my finger and said it would do until we could get to a jeweller's to choose a real engagement ring, a sapphire to match my eyes. You remember, don't you, Sam?'

CHAPTER TWO

'Is THIS your idea of a joke?' Sam grimly asked, staring at her as if she had grown another head. 'Because if it is I'm not amused.'

'Like Queen Victoria,' she murmured.

'What?' he snarled.

He was really furious, she realised, surprised. She had seen Sam angry before, but it had never been with her. He was far too possessed by his job, an energy-driven man, restless and obsessed. But all that fire went into his work, not his private life. With his women he was far more casual, very laid-back, making no commitments. He never seemed to take them seriously, and she knew none of his relationships lasted very long.

She had always been irritated by the way he treated his women, as if love was just a game. She suspected he thought of women as toys to pick up, play with and put down when you got bored. Natalie could never understand why women let him treat them that way. She wouldn't; that was for sure. Sam had once or twice asked her out, but she had always refused coolly. She only dated men who took her very seriously.

'She wasn't amused, either,' Natalie reminded him.

'Who wasn't?'

He seemed to be mentally challenged this morning, but that wasn't surprising after last night.

Patiently she repeated, 'Queen Victoria. Wasn't amused, remember?'

'I don't know what you're talking about!' he muttered.

Sam normally had a good sense of humour, but she let it pass, shrugging.

'Give me my ring and stop trying to be funny!' Sam stuck his hand out and she gazed at it without moving, opening her eyes as wide as she could.

'But, Sam, we're engaged to be married...'

He exploded, his voice going up several octaves. 'We are nothing of the kind and you know it! Okay, maybe I was so drunk last night that I somehow or other said something or other about—'

He broke off, having lost whatever he had been going to say, or perhaps not wishing to admit he had ever proposed to her. So Natalie ended the sentence for him.

'About marrying you? Yes, you did, Sam—in front of dozens of people. You proposed to me, on your...'

He loomed over her, smouldering. 'Yes, okay, I don't want to hear all that again. I was drunk. You know that! You know it wasn't serious!'

Of course she knew, but she wasn't ready to give up her game yet.

'But you asked me to marry you!' Her eyes opened wider than ever and he stared into the blueness of them for a few seconds, drawing a long, angry breath which he held as if he was counting to ten.

Then, in a very careful voice, he said, 'For heaven's sake, Natalie, we've never even had a date. Why should I suddenly propose out of the blue?'

'You said I was the perfect woman,' Natalie said in limpid tones. 'Your dream woman, you said.' She smiled mistily at him. 'It was very romantic—especially when you went on your knees and begged me to marry you.'

Sam stared at her, dark red creeping up his face. Running a hand through his already dishevelled hair, he muttered, 'You're kidding! I've never been that drunk before.'

Oh, thanks! she thought. That's really flattering.

Sam's brow corrugated. He's thinking at last! Natalie recognised. She hoped it hurt.

After a few seconds he groaned. 'It just dawned on me—was Helen there when I...?'

'Oh, yes,' said Natalie. In fact, she would never forget Helen West's face at that moment—it still made a glow in her memory. She had never liked the woman; not many people at the radio station did. The only people the singer was friendly to were youngish and good-looking men in good jobs. If you were poorer or older than her, or female, or plain, Helen West used you as a doormat or was coldly arrogant when she spoke to you—which was how she had always treated Natalie, who obviously came into most categories of people she despised.

'So that's why I got the slap in the face?' Sam fingered his jaw, grimacing. 'It still hurts.'

'Oh, poor Sam,' Natalie sweetly said, hoping it hurt a lot, and he looked down at her, his eyes now stiletto-sharp.

'You don't mean that, do you? If you did you'd want to kiss it better. As we're engaged!'

She blinked, startled. Why hadn't it dawned on her that he might do something like that? It should have done. She knew very well what an opportunist Sam was, in his work as well as in his private life.

Natalie wasn't the gambling type, but she took a gamble then, rather than abandon her little game with Sam, which she was enjoying too much to give up yet—although maybe her sense of humour was leading her into dangerous territory.

Lowering her lashes and looking at him through them, she murmured dulcetly, 'Bend down, then.'

She caught the flash of surprise in his eyes. He hadn't expected her to agree. But he bent, watching her as if wondering how far she was going to go, and Natalie lifted her head and pressed her mouth firmly on his jaw, more or less where Helen's slap had connected. His skin was cool and faintly prickly; he hadn't shaved as closely as usual this morning. In a hurry, no doubt, or his hand not too steady after the night before.

Natalie quickly moved away again. 'There. All better,' she mocked.

It might have been wiser not to say anything. She saw his grey eyes glint dangerously, then his hand shot out to capture her chin and hold it in position while his gaze roamed over her face with cool appraisal, as if he had never really noticed how she looked before. He probably hadn't, either. He was always too busy with work, or other women. She was just part of his office furniture, a useful piece of living equipment he needed for his job. Natalie was aware that she didn't come into the range of women Sam noticed sexually, and it had often annoyed her. Nobody liked being mistaken for a desk or a chair.

So, when he grabbed her chin and looked at her that way, she was ready to resent it—except that as she looked into his eyes pulses began to beat in her throat, at her wrist, a reaction that disturbed her. What was going on here? She had no designs on Sam, and she wasn't fool enough to let herself fall for him. She had thought it would be fun to tease him a little, that was all; getting involved with him had definitely not been in her game plan. Maybe it was time to stop playing with him before he began playing with her?

Oh, yes, definitely, she thought in agitation as she saw his gaze lingering on her mouth.

'Did I kiss you when I proposed?' he murmured in a smoky, deliberately sensuous tone that seemed to turn her brains to scrambled egg.

She gazed back at him, swallowing convulsively and unable to get a word out.

'I must have done,' he added. 'If I proposed. I must have kissed you, mustn't I? Pity I don't remember doing it. I'd like to remember that.'

His gaze was still riveted on her mouth. She felt her face growing hot and tried to say something, anything, to break the strange trance holding her rigid.

Sam bent. Slowly. Very slowly. Her mouth dry, Natalie stared up at his approaching face like a rabbit hypnotised by the dropping shadow of a bird of prey.

When his mouth touched her lips her body seemed to be set on fire; she was so stunned by her own feelings that she didn't even try pushing him away. She just shook like a leaf, her legs giving under her, her head falling back as if her neck had lost every bone in it and could no longer keep her head upright.

Sam's arms went round her waist as if to catch her; she clutched at him to keep herself standing on her own two feet. She had once been in an earthquake, in Turkey. This was just how it had felt: the same sense of helplessness, the feeling that you were no longer standing on ground you could trust, tremors running through you and shaking you to your roots.

His hands on the small of her back pushed her closer, closer, until she was lying against his bare chest, feeling the warmth of his skin through her own shirt and shivering at the intimacy of the contact, aware of every muscle in his body, every smooth, tanned inch of flesh. She was overwhelmed by a desire to bury her face in that beautiful male skin and was horrified by the impulse.

She must be out of her mind! What did she think she was doing, letting him do this to her? Pulling her head back from his kiss, she put her hands flat on that strong, naked chest, and shoved him away.

'Stop it!'

He looked down at her with half-hooded, drowsy eyes, as if waking up, and Natalie's heart skidded a dangerous corner. So was that how he looked first thing in the morning, in bed?

What are you thinking? she asked herself, despairing of her own brain. You told him to stop it—you should have told yourself the same thing!

Then Sam grinned down at her, mockery glinting in his face. 'But, Natalie, we're engaged, aren't we?'

'Oh, you think you're so funny!' she muttered. Well, it was her own fault for starting this game—she should have remembered that he was a tricky opponent; if you played games with Sam you had to do so with your eyes wide open, and his kiss had tricked her into closing hers. Maybe that was why she had gone a little crazy? Next time she'd keep her eyes wide open.

What next time? she asked herself furiously. There was never going to be another time, thank you very much. Once burnt, twice shy. She wasn't going within an inch of him in future. She had learnt something this morning that worried her.

Sam could get to her. If he got too close he could make her go crazy. Well, he wasn't getting another chance to do that to her!

His ring was a little loose on her finger, anyway; her fingers were so much smaller, thinner than his—so it was time she gave it back to him, in case she lost it. She would hate to do that, even if he richly deserved it. She knew how much the ring meant to him and his family, and how valuable it was.

'Here,' she said, very flushed, pulling the ring off and handing it to him.

'Jilting me so soon?' he reproached, but she noticed he accepted the ring without a second's hesitation and immediately slid it back onto his own finger with an audible sigh of relief.

'You know we weren't really engaged!' Natalie told him crossly, resenting his eagerness to get his ring back. 'I didn't take you seriously last night; I knew you were out of your head. I only kept your ring because I thought you might lose it if I didn't take care of it. You obviously had no idea what you were doing! I just hope it has taught you a lesson. Maybe next time you go to a party you won't drink so much.'

He eyed her coldly. 'Yes, Miss—thank you, Miss!' Then he grimaced. 'No, you're right—I can assure you, I will make sure I never drink that much again. I have the worst headache of my life today.'

'You deserve it,' she muttered, moving away.

He looked sharply at her, and then, his voice holding soft threat, said, 'Be careful, Natalie. Don't push it too far. Remember, I'm your boss. Now, would you be good enough to finish doing up my shirt?'

The last thing she wanted to do was go any closer to him again, but after being reminded that he was her employer she was wary of refusing point-blank—especially as those hard eyes of his were daring her to argue.

Also, if she refused she would betray something to him. He would realise she was afraid to come near him and he would start thinking about that and jumping to conclusions she didn't want him to jump to—conclusions she had only just begun to suspect herself and needed time to think through.

So without a word she did what he wanted, trying to avoid contact with any part of his body, gingerly pushing the buttons through the buttonholes without touching the bare skin under his shirt. She had to stand far too close to him for comfort, but she kept her eyes lowered all the time to avoid meeting his watchful gaze. Through her lashes she could see Sam's face, though, his eyes far too probing and thoughtful.

What was he thinking? Don't even wonder! she told herself. Better not to know. For her own peace of mind!

As soon as the last button was done up she quickly moved away, aware that her face was very pink and her throat beating with awareness. She was going to have to watch herself in future, whenever Sam was around. Since when had he had this effect on her, and why hadn't she noticed it until now?

You know why, she thought. This is the first time he's come so close, the first time he's made any sort of serious pass. He had once or twice tried to date her, when they'd first started working together, but she had turned him down cold and he had accepted that, had perhaps even been relieved—especially once they had worked together for a few weeks and Sam had realised she was so useful to him. Far too useful, in fact, for Sam to risk upsetting their working relationship by trying to seduce her.

That was why she hadn't been exposed to his particular brand of masculinity before—and, judging by the women she had seen him date over the three years since she'd begun working at the radio station, he was sexual dynamite. So why was she surprised that she had gone down with such worrying symptoms? She should have expected it. Why on earth had she run the risk of playing with fire?

Maybe if she kept her head and never got too close again she would get over this weird, dizzy weakness every time she looked at him—if she could do that, she might even be immunised for life.

'Shall we do some work now?' she asked him. 'We've got all these letters to deal with, and you have some calls to make.'

'Tell me, when did I start working for you?' Sam coldly enquired, lifting one black eyebrow. 'I had the distinct impression it was the other way around.'

She had had enough of playing games, so she shrugged casually. 'Oh, well, if you don't need me I might as well take my coffee break now.' In fact, she was relieved at the thought of getting away from him for a while.

She turned to walk to his office door but Sam moved into her path, dauntingly big and determined, obviously, to be very difficult.

'I've only just got here! We have a lot to do this morning. You're not taking any coffee breaks until I say so.'

'I thought you had decided not to work today!'

'I didn't say that—I told you I was your boss, you weren't mine. I decide what work we do. Before we deal with the mail I want to see last month's ratings, so would you ring AR and ask if they're ready?'

They had arrived that morning, from the audience research team, and she had known he would want to see them at once so she had put them on his desk along with the opened letters. Leaning over, she picked up the red folder and silently offered it to him.

Sam shot her a look like a knife that went right

through her and came out in her back. 'Has anyone ever told you how irritating you can be?'

'Yes, you, Mr Erskine—at least once a day since I started working for you.' She gave him another of her sweet, reasonable smiles. 'But you don't offend me, don't worry.' He could insult her all he liked while she was being paid so well to put up with him. 'It comes with the job,' she said. 'Like having to answer abusive phone calls from the listeners.'

Sam's teeth snapped tightly, as if he was biting off some furious comment, and she took a step back from him, not liking the glitter in his eyes. But luckily at that moment the office door crashed open and they both jumped and looked round, startled to see Johnny Linklater posing in the doorway, silver-lensed sunglasses hiding his eyes, his corn-coloured hair flopping carelessly over his temples. He had probably spent half an hour to get it to fall just like that. His image was his life's work. He left nothing to chance, even the fall of a lock of hair.

'Pinch me—see if you can find a pulse,' he said with dramatic melancholy as he strolled elegantly over to sink into the nearest chair. 'Am I alive or not? I can't quite decide.'

'Black coffee coming up,' Natalie said, picking up her cue and immediately going off to her own office to make it.

'You read my mind! Angel, darling heart, I love you,' Johnny called after her, and she smiled warmly at him.

He had arrived at precisely the right time and she was grateful to him for that. He had rescued her from what might have become a real problem with Sam, and it didn't help to acknowledge that it was her own fault. She had put ideas into Sam's head, ideas she did not want there, but how was she going to make him forget them?

She came back with the coffee a few moments later to find Johnny totally relaxed, lying back in his chair, propping his silver cowboy boots on Sam's desk, those long legs of his tightly encased in his usual black leather jeans. Johnny lived his own legend; he was never seen except dressed as if for a photo opportunity and he made sure he was usually surrounded by adoring fans, all of them female, most of them half his age, as if the proximity of the young might rub off on him, give him the illusion of youth for a few more years.

Natalie put the strong black coffee down on the desk, at his elbow, and he gave her a lazy smile, brushing back that soft flop of blond hair in a way that made it fall back precisely into place a second later.

'Thanks, honey. Did you enjoy my party? There were so many people there I didn't get to dance with you, and I'd promised myself I would, but things got so hectic. It was one of the best parties I've ever had, I thought.' There was a slight anxiety in his eyes, a question mark; under Johnny's apparent carelessness there was always this uncertainty, the melancholy of a man whose whole life depended upon his looks, which he knew to be finite.

'Everyone had a wonderful time, Johnny,' Natalie quickly assured him. 'I know I did; thank you for inviting me.'

'My pleasure, sweetheart.' Johnny's hooded eyes wandered down over her trim figure approvingly, then his face changed and, swinging his feet down from Sam's desk, he said, 'Hey, I just remembered. You could have knocked me down with a feather when you proposed, Sam—and I'll never forgive you for stealing the girl I had my eye on!' Bending his long, slim body, he lightly kissed Natalie on the cheek. 'I wish you every happiness, honey, and if he doesn't make you happy, give me a buzz and I'll come round and beat him up. Just say the word.'

Natalie slid a glance sideways at Sam, who was scowling. Let him explain to Johnny that there was no engagement! Why should she?

Cheerfully Johnny asked, 'When's the wedding? Better make it soon. The autumn schedules are pretty heavy—Sam's going to be very busy once we hit August. Hey, can I be best man? After all, you got engaged at my party?'

Sam said coldly, 'Thanks for the congratulations, but we aren't engaged, Johnny. It was just a joke.'

Johnny's jaw dropped. He looked into Sam's face, frowning, then at Natalie. 'Just a joke? Whose joke? Yours, Sam?' He was watching Natalie intently, his eyes searching her face. 'Did you know it was just a joke, honey?'

She was touched by the serious look in his face— Johnny might give the impression to most people that he was a playboy, flippant and shallow, but there was a serious side to him, hidden away.

'You don't honestly imagine I would ever consider marrying Sam?' She lightly shrugged, pretending to laugh. 'Of course I didn't take him seriously. I know he's not the marrying type, and even if he was, he's not *my* type.'

Johnny roared with laughter.

Sam was not so amused. In fact, when she risked a brief, sideways look at him, his face was icily blank—a fact which did not escape Johnny, either.

'This girl's smart; she's really got you figured out,' Johnny told him with a certain enjoyment. There had always been an element of friendly competition between the two men where women were concerned. Johnny put his arm round Natalie's waist. 'So I'm still in there with a chance, sweetheart?'

She let his arm stay where he had put it, and smiled at him without answering.

Sam said curtly, 'Have you noticed the time, Johnny? You should be in the studio getting your discs set up for the show by now, shouldn't you? Panic bells will be ringing in the control room if you don't show up soon.'

Instantly agitated, Johnny looked at his watch. 'God, you're right! I must run. See you both.' Carrying his mug of black coffee in one hand, he rushed out, letting the office door slam shut. Sam walked round his desk and sat down, tapping his long fingers on the wooden surface.

Giving Natalie a long, hard stare, he said, 'If you have any sense at all you won't start dating Johnny. He isn't your type, you know.'

'I'll be the judge of that!' Natalie couldn't agree more, in fact. She liked Johnny very much, but she wasn't sexually attracted to him. All the same, she wasn't having Sam dictating her private life. Give the man an inch and he was the type to take a mile—a real little office Napoleon. Either his mother had brought him up believing he was God's gift to the female sex, or he had an over-abundance of testosterone.

'Women have no judgement whatever where men are concerned!' Sam informed her.

She looked at him drily. 'Oh, I have a pretty shrewd idea what makes you tick.'

'Do you indeed?' he drawled, his mouth ironic. 'I doubt it. But I wasn't talking about myself. You know what I meant. Johnny Linklater is a great guy, and a buddy of mine, but I wouldn't trust him with one of my sisters.'

Natalie smiled at that, believing him. She knew Sam worried about his two younger sisters; it was one of his more endearing qualities. She knew, too, that his mother hen attitude drove both of them mad. They had confided in her one day a few months back, asking her how they could get him to stop trying to run their lives for them. Natalie had advised them that their wisest course was not to tell Sam anything they thought he might not like, although she couldn't help thinking that they should be more grateful for the care and concern Sam had always given them both.

Sam had been standing in for their dead father for years and he had got the habit, hadn't yet realised that Jeanie and Marie had grown up. They were both over twenty now; they had a right to make their own decisions, choose their own boyfriends, live their own lives.

'Just watch it with Linklater. The man's chronically unfaithful and completely irresponsible,' Sam said tersely.

'I've been looking after myself since I was sixteen,' said Natalie. 'I can manage Johnny, don't worry.'

Sam laughed angrily. 'Famous last words! A lot of other women have thought they could manage Johnny, but they all failed. Oh, well, if you want to make a fool of yourself I can't stop you—let's get down to work.' He reached for the audience research figures, his face set like concrete.

Natalie sighed—now he was going to be in a sulky mood all day, was he? Why were men so childish?

They spent half an hour going through the figures, then they moved on to skim through the mail; Sam dictated a few letters in reply, before starting on a memo to be sent to all the production offices on keeping costs down and using studios more economically and efficiently. It was one he sent out every few months. At first people were very careful, but slowly standards would slip and back would creep all the bad habits into which big organisations slid if nobody kept an eye on them.

He was halfway through dictating his memo when the phone rang and he picked it up. 'Hello? Yes, speaking.' He looked startled. 'Oh, hello, Jeanie—anything wrong? What? No, I haven't seen any of this morning's papers.' His voice shot up to a roar, making Natalie jump. 'What? Said what?' he yelled into the phone.

There was a silence while he listened, his face darkening, his eyes glittering with temper, then he said, 'No, it isn't! Of course not. She what? Oh, my God. Well, tell her it was all just a joke. No, you tell her. If I ring her she'll keep asking me stupid questions and probing like a dentist... Well, I know she worries about me, she's always telling me she does, but... No, I won't ring her. I want you to do it. Are you listening, Jeanie? Hello? Jeanie?'

He slammed the phone down and stared at it as if it were a snake. 'Damn. She hung up on me.'

'What's wrong?' asked Natalie.

He looked at her with grim eyes. 'They've heard about last night. It's all your fault!'

The injustice took her breath away. When she got it back she burst out in a muddled flood of words. 'It wasn't me who got drunk and proposed to me! It wasn't me who gave me his signet ring and insisted I wear it!'

'It's your job to keep me out of trouble. That's what I pay you for!' he snapped at her, like a piranha lunging for a meal.

She snapped right back at him. 'Oh, and all this time

I thought I was hired as your secretary, not your keeper! Silly me. Remind me to change the job description when I advertise for my successor tomorrow!'

'What?' He looked taken aback, his brows jerking together in a scowl.

'I'm handing in my notice!' she said, reckless enough at that moment to jump off the top of the building. She didn't want to leave, of course; she certainly hadn't planned to go. She loved her job, loved working at the radio station—her work was so various and stimulating, she never knew what she would be doing each morning when she came into work. She hated to admit it but she even loved working with Sam, except when he was in a bad mood; he was a good boss, he trusted her, left her with plenty of responsibility. She liked that, enjoyed the equality they usually shared. He let her speak her mind; he listened. They had a good relationship.

But since last night everything was different. He had changed the atmosphere between them—or had she? No, it was down to both of them. Last night it had been Sam who'd behaved badly, but she had been stupid to take the game so far this morning. She should just have given him back his ring and let the matter drop. Why had she been so stupid? Now everything had become too personal, too charged, and Natalie couldn't cope with it. She wanted to get away.

Sam glowered at her. 'We've had enough bad jokes for one day, Natalie!'

'I'm not joking. I'm resigning. As of today,' she told him, and got up to walk out. But Sam got up too, uncoiling that long, powerful body and making her back away. There was a sense of threat about him when he looked at you like that. Anyone with any sense got out of his way.

'You're doing nothing of the kind!' he said through his teeth. 'I need you.'

Her heart flipped at the words—what did he mean by that? Was he admitting that...? But then Sam went on talking, and her heart slowed again.

'You've got to talk to my mother!' he told her fiercely. 'According to Jeanie, she's planning some big party to celebrate our engagement. She's even working out where we should get married, and when, and how many guests we ought to have. You must ring her at once and put a stop to it.'

Natalie was aghast. 'How on earth did your mother find out about last night?'

'Jeanie says it was in a gossip column. Somebody at the party must have rung a paper. If I ever find out who did it...'

'There were some press people at the party.' Natalie groaned, her heart sinking. 'I'd forgotten them. They were mostly columnists, too. Entertainment reporters and gossip columnists. Oh, why did you have to drink so much?'

'I'm turning teetotal, don't worry!' Sam curtly said. 'But never mind that now—I want you to ring my mother at once.'

'Why me? It isn't my problem. She's your mother—you ring her.' Natalie was indignant; he had made this muddle, it was up to him to get himself out of it. It certainly wasn't her fault and she did not see why she should have to do his dirty work for him.

He made a face. 'She'll blame me and—'

'You are to blame!'

He didn't like the reminder, she saw that from his eyes—Sam had a low threshold where blame was concerned—but he used a soothing voice, trying to placate her, anything to get her to do what he asked. 'I know, I know, but she's going to get upset, and I can't cope with my mother when she's upset. She'll start worrying about you—have I hurt your feelings? How could I do that to a nice girl like you? I should be ashamed of myself—' He broke off, seeing her expression, and gave her a sulky look. 'All right, all right. I admit she could have a point. I've apologised once, Natalie—how many more times do I have to do it?'

'I didn't notice you doing any apologising. You seemed to think it was my fault, not yours.'

'Well, I apologise now. How's that? I'm sorry. Okay? Now, please ring my mother—if you talk to her she'll realise you haven't got a broken heart. If you tell her it was all just a joke and you never for a second thought it was serious, you knew it was just fun and the Press got it all wrong, she'll believe you. Especially if you're cheerful and keep laughing.' He looked at her through those thick black lashes. 'And, after all, you said yourself you knew it was a joke and you never took it seriously. Didn't you? So it won't be a problem for you—you'll only be telling the truth, won't you?'

She gave him a dry look. He never missed a trick, did he? That was what made him such a brilliant organiser. That was why the radio station ticked along like a well-made clock. 'Okay,' she sighed. 'I'll ring her.'

'Now, please,' he said—before she could change her mind, he meant!

Natalie had his mother's number in her computer. She dialled at once, wishing Sam wouldn't hover like that; she could feel his agitation without looking at him. The phone rang and rang without anyone picking it up. 'Nobody in,' she said at last, hanging up.

'I wonder where on earth she can be?' Sam rhetori-

cally asked her. His mouth turned down at the edges.
'And what she's up to! Once my mother gets an idea in
her head she wastes no time. She loves organising parties. If we don't stop her in time she'll have sent out
dozens of invitations and spent a fortune, and it will be
expensive and embarrassing putting a stop to it.'

Natalie watched him without saying, this time, what
she was thinking. She had told him it served him right
several times already—no point in rubbing it in. Poor
Sam. He wouldn't forget Johnny's party in a hurry,
would he?

CHAPTER THREE

NATALIE'S lunch hour began at one o'clock, but when she looked at the clock at five to one and said, 'Nearly lunchtime!' Sam glowered at her.

'If there's one thing I can't stand it's clock-watching secretaries!'

He was still in a bad temper, but Natalie pretended not to notice. 'I'm not clock-watching—I was reminding you that you've got a lunch appointment yourself. Had you forgotten?'

'It's been cancelled.' He shrugged. 'Hugh Sartfield's secretary rang while you were doing those letters. Hugh has got mumps.'

Natalie couldn't help laughing; there was something comical about the mere idea of mumps, although she knew it could be very painful.

Sam gave her a cold stare. 'You wouldn't think that was funny if you were a man!'

Sobering, Natalie nodded. 'Sorry, yes, I know it can be serious for adults—poor Mr Sartfield. Let's hope he doesn't get any long-term effects.'

'I spent a couple of hours with him only last week,' Sam said, his hand rubbing one side of his face. 'Mumps is very contagious, isn't it? I wonder when the infectious period starts?'

'I should ring your doctor,' Natalie said, getting up.

'I think I will. Hey, where do you think you're going?'

'Lunch.' She wanted to get away before he could stop her, but in her hurry she tripped over her chair and couldn't stop herself sprawling helplessly across the carpet. To her fury she heard Sam laugh, then he bent, put an arm round her waist and hauled her to her feet.

'That will teach you not to be in such a hurry!' he said, still holding her, looking down into her face.

The fall must have knocked all the breath out of her body; she could feel her heart driving like a steamhammer inside her chest. She couldn't meet his gaze; she simply pulled free from him. The last thing she wanted was for Sam to think she was flushed and breathing fast because of him! It was only the shock of falling over. Nothing to do with him at all.

She had dropped her bag when she fell. Bending to pick it up, she crossly realised that she had made an enormous run in her tights, right down the front from her knee to her slender ankle.

'Oh, no!' she muttered. She couldn't go around with a run like that in her tights for the rest of the day. Before she went down to the canteen for lunch she would have to go out to buy some new tights.

'What's the matter?' Sam asked, looking down at her legs. 'You've got a run in—'

'I know,' she said curtly. 'Can I go to lunch now?'

'Oh, very well! But be back on time!'

She didn't bother to answer that. It was already ten past one; she was taking her full hour, whether he liked it or not.

There was a useful corner shop just across the street, which did a good line in cheap tights. Although Natalie was well-paid she had learnt thrift at her mother's knee and was always looking for ways to save money. She needed to; she had a mortgage on a small studio flat whose windows looked down over the harbour. That took far too much of her monthly salary and Natalie had to budget carefully where clothes and food were concerned. She never bought anything without being sure she couldn't get it cheaper somewhere else.

Emerging two minutes later, tights safely stowed in her jacket pocket, Natalie ran back to the radio station as a car, a little red Ford saloon, drew up outside. Not even glancing at it, Natalie hurried past, intending to change her tights in the powder room next door to the canteen, only to stop in her tracks as someone called her.

'Natalie!'

She spun, her sleek dark hair swinging against her cheeks, and felt her stomach sink as she recognised the woman emerging from the red car. Her once dark hair silvery, her figure no longer quite so slim, although she dressed in a traditionally elegant fashion that made a tendency to weight less obvious, Mrs Erskine was still a very attractive woman.

She had lost her husband when Sam was only sixteen—why had she never married again? Natalie wondered vaguely as she said, 'Hello, Mrs Erskine! Sam has been trying to get in touch with you all morning!'

Tartly, Sam's mother said, 'I should think so, too! He ought to be ashamed of himself. Why did I have to hear about your engagement from someone else? He should have rung me first thing this morning! I tried ringing him but there was never any reply.'

But she smiled, too, and for the first time Natalie realised that her eyes were almost identical to Sam's, a brighter grey, perhaps, yet the shape of them exactly the same. The bone structure of her face was more delicate, but there was a strong similarity in the way their eyebrows had that winged angle and the way they both smiled.

Putting an arm around Natalie, Mrs Erskine kissed her warmly on both cheeks. 'But it's wonderful, Natalie! I couldn't be more pleased. If he had let me choose a girl for him it would have been someone just like you! He has gone out with some quite appalling girls in the past, but Sam's taste has obviously improved!'

Laughing, flattered, secretly very touched, but knowing she had to quickly get in her explanation, Natalie stammered, 'That's very nice of you, Mrs Erskine, but…'

'My dear, I mean every word of it!'

Flushed, Natalie said, 'Thank you, but I'm afraid you've got the wrong impression…you see, it isn't true—'

She never got to finish the sentence. Mrs Erskine interrupted again, laughing. 'Of course it is, Natalie! You're perfect for him. You've been the perfect secretary; he says so himself. Whatever sort of fool Sam has always been where women were concerned, at least he had the good sense to value you! And so did we… Me and my girls, Jeanie and Marie, we said to each other when we first met you that you would make Sam a wonderful wife, but we never dared hope he'd have the sense to ask you. I'm so thrilled that he finally did.'

She paused, and, pink as a geranium, Natalie sadly told her, 'I'm sorry, Mrs Erskine, but we're not…not engaged. It was just a joke last night, at the party, you see—we're not engaged at all.'

Mrs Erskine stared back at her incredulously. 'Not?'

Natalie shook her head, looking away. 'I'm afraid not,' she said, wishing she were somewhere else. Why had she let Sam talk her into breaking the news to his mother?

'But it said in the newspaper…' Mrs Erskine seemed to be having a problem taking it in.

Natalie sighed. 'I know, there were some press people at the party—we had forgotten they were there—they weren't in on the joke. They took it seriously…they thought it was for real…but we were just having fun and…'

'Fun!' Mrs Erskine erupted furiously. 'I don't see anything funny at all. I've just spent the morning organising a party for you—an engagement party. I've rung dozens of people…friends, relatives…and caterers, and ordered flowers and a big cake, and booked at the hotel… Hours of work, talking on the phone, driving around to see people! And now you tell me it was just a joke!'

Natalie whispered, 'I'm so sorry.' If Sam had appeared at that moment she thought she would have hit him with something very hard. How dared he do this to her? This was his mother, he had caused the problem—why was Natalie having to cope with the consequences?

'Sorry!' Mrs Erskine looked at her with rage in her eyes. 'Sorry! What good is an apology to me? You've made me look a complete idiot, both of you. Everything is organised…' She put both hands to her hair as if she was about to pull it out by the roots. 'Oh, heavens, what on earth am I supposed to do? Ring everyone back and say, Sorry, it was just a joke? Everything is cancelled, just forget it? Do you really think they…the hotel, the florist, the caterer—any of them…are going to be amused?'

Put like that, Natalie could think of nothing to say. She bit her lip, gazing at Sam's mother with embarrassed sympathy.

'They will probably demand that I compensate them for their disappointment. A cancellation fee is quite usual these days, to stop people wasting their time—and I could hardly blame them if they suspected me of being a silly time-waster, now, could I?'

Feebly, Natalie murmured soothingly, 'I'm sure they'll understand when you explain.'

'Of course they won't! It's going to be very awkward making all these calls—quite apart from the time wasted on both sides. I'm going to feel very small.'

Before she could stop herself, Natalie said, 'I'll ring them and explain! This afternoon, from the office—and as to any cancellation fees, well, if there are, Sam can pay. This is all his fault, anyway. Let him pay.'

She couldn't keep a note of bitterness out of her voice and his mother looked sharply and thoughtfully at her.

'You're right! Let him pay!' she slowly said, then looked at her watch. 'I tell you what, Natalie, let's go and have lunch somewhere nice—how about the Sea King's Cave, that seafood restaurant down on the harbour? Their seafood platter is delicious, and brilliantly presented on crushed ice with seaweed dressing—I love it, and so low-calorie, too. We can have lunch and talk, make out the list of people who must be rung immediately—all the professional people. I'll deal with the family and the friends myself. I couldn't ask you to make those calls.'

'I'd love to, but Sam wants me back in the office by two, and there wouldn't be time, I'm afraid,' Natalie regretfully told her, glancing at her own watch. Twenty past one now! She would have to rush just to have lunch in the canteen—let alone eat down at the harbour.

'Who cares what Sam wants? As you said, this is all his fault. If he gets difficult you refer him to me! I know how to deal with Sam!' Mrs Erskine was in a belligerent mood, her usually soft, smiling eyes sparkling with temper.

Natalie thought about it. Sam would undoubtedly explode into little tiny pieces all over the office if she didn't come back to work in time—which, now she thought about it, was one very good reason for taking up his mother's invitation.

Mrs Erskine turned back to her car, unlocking the door. 'Get in, Natalie!' she ordered, with something of her son's casual authority, and after a pause Natalie obeyed.

As they drove off Sam emerged from the building behind them and stopped in his tracks, staring after the car. Natalie caught sight of him in the wing mirror and was enchanted by the worried expression on his face. He must be wondering what on earth was going on, why she was driving off with his mother! Well, good. Let him worry.

Before they turned a corner to drive on down towards the sea she saw Sam walk towards the pub where he often ate his lunch. He usually had a Ploughman's Platter: a mixture of Cheddar and Gloucester cheese, sliced crusty bread and butter, and some crisp salad, with which Sam drank a glass of beer. He was a creature of habit, so no doubt that was what he would be eating today. She hoped it gave him the worst indigestion he had ever had in his life. The amusement with which she had begun the day had long gone; now she was beginning to be angry with him. She had a difficult and embarrassing afternoon ahead of her, making a string of phone calls to cancel the party his mother had organised, and it was all Sam's fault.

There were other reasons why she was so angry with him, but she pushed them to the back of her mind. This morning she had made a few worrying discoveries about herself and her own feelings—but this was neither the time nor the place to investigate them. She would do that when she was alone, at home, with no watching eyes to read her face.

When they arrived at the restaurant they were given a table in the vast plate glass window, with a wonderful view of the harbour—multicoloured yachts tied up along the quayside, bobbing on the water, their mast wires rattling in a little breeze, holidaymakers strolling along in summery clothes, the sun glittering on blue waves, white gulls flying overhead. Natalie rarely had a chance to enjoy the picturesque nature of the little seaside town where she lived; there wasn't enough time during the week and at weekends she had her housework, cooking and washing to do. Her life was far too busy, she realised, gazing out with pleasure.

The seafood Mrs Erskine had talked about proved to be as delicious as she had promised, and Natalie enjoyed the glass of ice-cool champagne they had with their meal.

As she took her first sip of it Sam's mother said, 'Where do your family live, Natalie? Here, in town? Are you a local girl?'

Natalie nodded. 'Yes, I grew up here. We lived in a house in the old part of town. But since my father retired my parents have moved to a bungalow ten miles away. My mother has arthritis and was finding the stairs a problem.'

She forked up a scallop and dipped it into a pale pink sauce, one of the dips which had been served in small, matching bowls with the big oval platter of seafood and a large bowl of salad.

Mrs Erskine was swallowing an oyster, which she had dipped into a hot chilli sauce Natalie had already tried and found far too spicy for her taste. Mrs Erskine must have a mouth lined with asbestos! Natalie watched her with respect.

'Are you an only child?' asked Mrs Erskine, and Natalie shook her head.

'No, I have an older sister, Bethany, five years older than me; she's married, with a two-year-old son, Harry.

She lives in London; her husband is a civil servant working in Whitehall.'

'Do you see much of your parents?'

'I visit them every week, usually on Sunday afternoon, for tea. My father and I take the dog for a walk over the downs behind their bungalow, along a public footpath which has a great view, then when we get back I help Mum lay the table while Dad watches sport on television—so I get a chance to talk to each of them alone.'

'That's nice.'

They ate in silence for a few minutes, then, when they had finished their seafood, Mrs Erskine asked, 'Would you like a pudding, my dear?'

'I couldn't eat another morsel,' Natalie said, smiling at her. 'Thank you, that was a marvellous meal.'

'I'm glad you enjoyed it. Coffee?'

'I'd love one, thank you.' Natalie glanced at her watch, though, slightly guilty as she saw it was now half past two. Catching his mother's eye, she grimaced. 'Sam will think I've taken the day off!'

'Who cares what Sam thinks? Tell me more about yourself—do you have any hobbies?'

'I play tennis and badminton, and I enjoy going to the local repertory theatre if they're doing a play I like. And if I get the time I like to paint.'

Mrs Erskine sat up, eyes interested. 'So do I! What a coincidence! Oils or...?'

'Watercolours. And I like to work in charcoal—black and white sketches.' Hurriedly, Natalie protested, 'I'm not very good! It is just a hobby.'

'Do you paint indoors, or out?'

'That depends on the weather. I prefer to paint in the open air; the light is always better and I like to be out of doors. I've done a few paintings down here, actually, on the harbour wall—and sometimes I paint on the downs behind my parents' bungalow.'

'You must come and paint in our garden—you know we have a house at Abbotslea, right on the cliff. Our views across the downs are magnificent. I often paint them. I'd enjoy having someone else painting nearby. I have several easels; you could use one of them to save you the trouble of bringing your own.'

Natalie gave her a surprised, pleased smile. 'Thank you, I'd love to do that one day.'

'How about next Saturday? You said you go to your parents on a Sunday, but are you free this Saturday?'

'Well, yes, I am…' Natalie hesitated briefly. How would Sam feel about her visiting his mother? There had never been anything but a business relationship between Sam and herself—might he object to her becoming so friendly with his mother? More than likely! He might suspect her of trying to sneak some advantage. It was the traditional route, wasn't it, for girls pursuing a man—to make friends with his mother? If he even hinted at that idea, though, she would brain him. Maybe she shouldn't take up Mrs Erskine's invitation?

Watching her confused, uncertain face, Mrs Erskine laughed suddenly.

'Never mind what Sam will say!'

Natalie gave her a startled, flushed look. How had Mrs Erskine known what she was thinking? Natalie took a deep breath, smiling. 'I don't care what he says! I'd be very happy to come. Thank you.'

Mrs Erskine gave her an approving nod. 'Good for you. Come for lunch. If it is fine we'll eat out on the patio—just a salad and some cold salmon or chicken—then we'll set up our easels and paint.'

'Sounds wonderful!' Natalie hadn't painted much recently; she kept meaning to set up her easel but there was so much else to do. 'And if you let me have those numbers...the caterers and so on...I'll get those calls made this afternoon.'

'Sure?' Sam's mother searched her face with probing eyes. Natalie nodded, smiling at her, so Mrs Erskine fished in her handbag and produced a handwritten list. She tore off a strip at the bottom and handed it to Natalie. 'Then here you are, these are the phone numbers of the caterer, the florist, the hotel—and I'm very grateful to you for offering to ring them.'

'I'll do my level best to placate them,' Natalie promised. 'And I'll let you know how it goes.'

'Thank you, my dear.' Mrs Erskine sighed, ruefully glancing down the rest of the names on her list. 'And meanwhile I shall have to ring my friends and relatives. That isn't going to be easy—they may pretend to be sympathetic, but I know they'll all laugh at me behind my back. I shouldn't have been so quick off the mark. I should have waited until I'd talked to Sam. I'm afraid I've always been in a hurry with life. I can never bear to wait for anything. And Sam has kept me waiting for so long. I do so badly want to see him happily married.'

You'll be lucky! thought Natalie. Sam wasn't the marrying sort. He didn't believe in making a commitment; he knew marriage would put a stop to his carefree existence, to the girls, the fun, the freedom, the irresponsibility. Sam was a Peter Pan; he didn't want to grow up. But she didn't want to depress his mother so she didn't say that to her.

Ten minutes later they drove back to the radio station; Mrs Erskine dropped Natalie and drove off, waving. Natalie went up in the lift and walked into her own office to find Sam waiting for her, snorting like a fire-breathing dragon, his face angry, his tie off and his shirt collar undone, his jacket hung over the back of his chair and

his thick black hair tousled, dishevelled, as if he had
been running his hand through it for hours.

'Where the hell have you been?' he broke out as soon
as she appeared in the doorway. 'I saw you drive off
with my mother!'

'I know you did. I saw you too.'

He eyed her menacingly. 'Where were you going?'

'We had lunch together.'

'Lunch together?' he repeated, as if he was having
trouble with that concept.

'Yes. You know—we went to a restaurant, together,
and we had food, together,' Natalie gravely expanded.

His eyes flashed. 'You aren't funny, Natalie!' he
snarled, taking two strides and suddenly far too close for
comfort. She had never really noticed before what a very
physical presence he had; without even touching her he
made her dangerously aware of his body and every
breath she took.

Refusing to think about that, she lifted her chin and
looked back at him without blinking. 'I wasn't being
funny. We had lunch down at the harbour, at a marvellous seafood place. The Sea King's Cave, it's called. We
had a great platter of seafood: oysters and mussels and
scallops and prawns and—'

'Never mind what you ate!' he erupted, looming even
closer and making her nerves flicker with awareness.
'Why were you having lunch with my mother?'

'Because she invited me.'

He looked down at her as if he wanted to slap her,
and she wouldn't have been surprised to know that that
was exactly what he wanted to do. It was strange—they
had had a perfectly amicable relationship in the office
for three years, yet today everything felt different—as if
they were both on the verge of something dangerous,
two people on the very slopes of a volcano which might

blow at any minute. Natalie found it nerve-racking. Every time she'd been with him today she had felt the same edgy reaction, and she didn't like it.

'When did she invite you? Why didn't you tell me you were having lunch with her?'

'I didn't know I was going to—we met in the street and she said, "Come and have lunch with me," so I went.'

He considered that, still frowning blackly. 'Why did she do that?' he said, half to himself.

'I don't know. It was just a spur of the moment thing, I suppose.'

'Did you tell her that we're not engaged?' he demanded, and she gave him a cool nod.

'Yes, I told her.'

Sam gave a rough sigh of relief, then asked anxiously, 'How did she take it?'

He really cared about his mother and his sisters, and Natalie liked that part of his character; a man who cared about his family was the sort of man she wanted to marry. Not, she hurriedly thought, that she had Sam himself in mind; he was hardly the ideal man in other ways. She didn't like his temper, or his tendency to be dictatorial, or his...

'Well?' he snapped. 'Are you daydreaming? I asked you how my mother took the news?'

She opened her blue eyes at him. 'Well, she wasn't too happy about it, actually. She had organised a party— an engagement party...'

He groaned, turning pale.

Deliberately Natalie expanded. 'She had booked a hotel suite, caterers, a florist...'

'Oh, God,' Sam whispered.

'And she was very upset about having to *un*book them all,' Natalie finished.

'But she is going to?'

He was looking like a man on the edge of a cliff who thought he might be forced to jump. Did Sam fear that his mother wasn't going to cancel the engagement party? Was he scared of finding himself having to carry on with their phoney engagement? It was that big a nightmare, was it? He made her so angry, her hands screwed into fists at her sides. She would like to…

'What are you looking at me like that for?' Sam asked, and she gave him a chilly smile.

'Was I looking at you in any particular way? I wasn't aware of it.'

'Hmm,' he murmured. 'Well, whatever you're thinking, stop it, because you're making the hair stand up on the back of my neck.'

'Oh, dear, mustn't have that, must we?' she said in a barbed tone.

Sam paused, watching her shrewdly. 'I asked you…is my mother cancelling this party?'

'Well, no,' Natalie said coolly, and saw a look of witless panic come into his face.

'She…isn't? But she must! She can't go ahead with the party, and even if she did, I wouldn't go to it. Ring her and tell her that. I am not going to any engagement parties!'

'No need to get yourself into a state,' Natalie icily told him. 'There won't be any party. Your mother was dreading having to ring everyone and cancel, so I offered to do it for her. It will mean spending some time making phone calls this afternoon—she gave me a list.' She took it out of her bag and showed it to him. 'But you won't mind that, will you?' she ended pointedly. 'It will be such a relief to you.'

His eyes narrowed and flint-hard, he eyed her grimly. 'I see. You were playing another peculiar game of your own with me. I hadn't realised you had a vindictive streak, Natalie. You were teasing me to punish me for last night, weren't you? Typical female trick. You don't come out with what's on your mind, you just pay me back in your own way by making me sweat. Women! No wonder men can never understand them. They have minds like corkscrews. They smile sweetly and stick a knife in you without giving you any idea what you've done wrong.'

He knew perfectly well what he had done, but Natalie wasn't arguing with him. He was like an unexploded bomb; it wasn't wise to get too close.

So instead she softly asked him, 'Hadn't I better hurry up and make those phone calls? The sooner the better, I'd have thought.'

His skin was dark red with temper by now. He bit out through his teeth, 'Oh, get on with it! And don't take too long about it. When you've finished maybe we can get on with some work!'

'There's no need to talk to me like that!' Her own temper ran out of control suddenly. 'It wasn't me who—'

'We've been through all that!' snarled Sam. 'Okay, I'm responsible. I admit, it was all my fault. But I'm paying for it. This has been one of the most disastrous days of my life so far!'

Pain jabbed suddenly in Natalie's chest. So it had been a disastrous day for him, finding himself engaged to her, had it?

She was under no illusions about the way Sam regarded the idea of marriage, and she knew he would never in a million years have proposed to her, anyway—not if he had been sober. She wasn't his type. She didn't have the glamour and looks of the women Sam normally dated. He liked glossy, exciting women—and Natalie knew she wasn't one, just as she had known last night that his proposal wasn't genuine. She had gone along with it so as not to make a scene, and she had only let him put his ring on her finger in case he lost it. This morning she had meant to give it back to him. She wished she had now. She wished she hadn't been tempted to have a little fun at his expense.

It had backfired on her somehow. Sam was angry and Natalie had a strange aching around her heart, a depression centred on her like one of those black clouds they put up on the TV weather report. Playing games was dangerous. She wished she hadn't done it.

She went through to her office and sat down at her desk with Mrs Erskine's list. It took her an hour to make all the calls—one of the most embarrassing hours of her entire life. She did not identify herself as being one of the supposedly engaged couple, she simply said she was making the calls for Mrs Erskine—which left her exposed to some very frank comments from the people at the other end, who supposed she had no feelings to be hurt and said exactly what they thought about the cancellation.

The hotel manager was first furious, then laughed and said, 'So he wriggled out, did he? I thought it was too good to be true. Sam Erskine is one of nature's bachelors. He comes here all the time, with different girls; he certainly knows how to pick 'em. I wish I had his cast-offs, that's all! He'll never marry! And why should he? A man like him…it would be a waste!'

A man like Sam…it would be a nightmare for any woman stupid enough to marry him! thought Natalie. But the hotel manager was right about one thing—Sam would probably never marry; he had far too good a time staying out of matrimony.

The caterer was a woman, who complained bitterly

about the order being cancelled. 'I'll have to charge a cancellation fee! I've already ordered some of the items I would have needed.'

'Write to Mrs Erskine with the details, then, would you?' Natalie told her.

Then the caterer asked, 'What happened, anyway? Poor guy, I'm sorry for him—dumped so soon! What sort of cockroach is she, this girl? His mother was so excited, too, over the moon about her son finally getting married; she's dying to have grandchildren, she said. She must be very upset now. Some women simply don't care how much they hurt people, do they?'

'I don't think it was like that!' Natalie protested. She couldn't explain that there had never been a real engagement. She wasn't discussing anything so private with a total stranger.

The other woman snorted down the phone. 'Want to bet? I know my own sex, even if you don't. This girl probably got a better prospect. My brother was mad about this blonde last year; he asked her to marry him, gave her a diamond ring I'd give my eye teeth for, then she met a guy with a Rolls Royce and a detached home, dumped my brother and went off. But she never gave the ring back.'

'Well, I must go. Sorry again,' Natalie said in a voice choked with fury, and hung up, seething.

Sam had said this was one of the most disastrous days of his life. Well, snap. The same went for her, in spades.

She had begun the day with a feeling of amusement. She had looked forward to seeing Sam's face when he saw his ring on her finger. She had thought the whole episode was a great joke. Now she saw it very differently.

Something had happened to her today—something she hadn't expected, hadn't so much as dreamt about—and she wished feverishly that she could turn the clock back to last night, make it all happen differently, make sure Sam didn't drink too much, make sure he didn't propose to her or give her his ring. If none of that had happened she wouldn't have been tempted to tease him, pretend she believed they really were engaged.

Then Sam wouldn't have kissed her and she might never have realised she was already half in love with him.

CHAPTER FOUR

THE rest of that week dragged by minute by minute, hour by hour; Natalie had never known time to go so slowly. Yet she and Sam were just as busy as ever. People came and went in their office, they had the usual deluge of mail to cope with and the phone rang constantly. She shouldn't have noticed the passage of time at all; normally she never did. Only a week ago, she knew, she wouldn't have so much as looked at the clock except to think hectically, Oh, no, look at the time! And I've still got so much to do! Yet here she was, aware of every tick of the clock—not just the minutes but the seconds, slowly passing, every one of them a little thorn under her skin, making her bleed internally.

Sam's mood was even worse than hers. He said very little to her, except about work, and even then he almost seemed to hurl the words, his grey eyes flecked with ice and his face as grim as winter. Everyone at the radio station noticed Sam's permanent state of temper. They never commented on it to him, they didn't dare in case he turned on them and bit their heads off, but they muttered sideways remarks to Natalie.

'What's up with him?' one said. 'Who pulled his tail?'

And one of the engineers, after a tense session with Sam over a technical hitch during a long programme, which had resulted in a few seconds of silence on air, came out very red, muttering, 'If he talks to me that way again, I'll push his teeth through the back of his head!'

Ellie Corkhill, the girl who ran the advertising department, asked tentatively in the canteen on

Wednesday, 'Is Sam acting this way because you dumped him?' Then, on a breath, she sighed, 'He must be in a lot of pain, poor Sam—rejection can really hurt. I know.'

Everyone avoided looking at her because they all knew, too, that Ellie had recently been dumped by her boyfriend; she had talked about nothing else for weeks and often had the sheen of tears in her eyes.

Quickly another secretary, Kay Lincoln, asked with a sweet smile, 'We're all dying to know, Natalie—did you dump him, or was it really the other way round?'

'I never said I dumped him!' Natalie crossly told them. 'We got engaged at Johnny's party when we were both out of our heads, but when we sobered up we immediately got unengaged!'

Kay's eyes were a feline, almond-shaped green; they glittered with malice. 'So why's Sam been in such a bad mood ever since?'

'No idea. But it has nothing to do with me.'

'Oh, no? Then why have you been like a cat in a rainstorm lately?'

'I've been nothing of the kind!' Natalie gave Kay a freezing look.

It didn't seem to affect the other girl at all. In fact, she laughed, tossing back her short red hair and watching Natalie closely as she retorted, 'No? Could have fooled us. Of course Sam could be missing Helen West. She hasn't been seen with him since, either, has she? Poor Sam. He must be getting frustrated—all this time and no woman in his bed? Unless you know different? I mean, you two aren't playing house as well as working together in the office?'

Natalie didn't rise to it. She pushed her plate away and got up to go back to her office. The sooner the gossips found something else to talk about the better.

She wasn't sure, in fact, why Sam was so bad-tempered at the moment. Maybe his mother and sisters were giving him a hard time? The news of his engagement followed by a swift denial of it might have triggered a family row. Mrs Erskine had certainly been angry enough, upset enough, to tell Sam exactly what she thought of his behaviour, and Sam might well blame Natalie for that.

He obviously blamed her for something. While they were working together he avoided looking at her—and she found herself doing the same, which, in the confined space of the office, day in, day out, was not easy. They avoided getting too close, too, kept out of each other's body space. She felt as if Sam was surrounded by an electric force field which might damage her if she collided with it. Just being within inches of him made her aware of the vibrating power of that electricity; she could almost see the sparks coming off him, and each time she would hurriedly move away. She suspected Sam felt the same.

He would pace the room while he was talking to her, and now and then come close to her, only to swing away, sharply, like a tiger in a cage coming up against the bars, and without looking at her stride to the other side of the room.

The nervous tension ate at her more and more as the week went on; she couldn't wait for the weekend and a couple of days away from him.

On Thursday she was eating in the canteen when Johnny Linklater came over with his tray and asked if he could sit at her table.

'Of course you can!' She felt the stir of excitement in the canteen and smiled to herself. Whenever Johnny came into the canteen he got the same reaction.

Some of the younger girls were as crazy about Johnny

as his fans were, although it was a radio station unwritten rule that staff did not bother the famous who came in to make programmes. That didn't stop girls gazing at Johnny with their hearts in their eyes. If he had wanted to, he could have picked up any of them merely by crooking his little finger. They would come running, and no doubt he knew it, but Sam disapproved of company affairs; it made for trouble. Other girls would be jealous, and if Johnny tired of a relationship and broke it off there would be tears and tantrums, and work would suffer. So Johnny normally did not date any of the girls who worked at the radio station.

Johnny had a salad, the same one Natalie had picked out—a little mound of cottage cheese dressed with crushed pineapple and fresh local cherries on a bed of green leaves, lettuce and watercress and endive, cucumber and some strips of green pepper.

He picked up a glass of sparkling mineral water from his tray. 'Cheers, darling!' he said, clinking the ice against the glass. 'See? I'm on the wagon, like Sam.'

'Is he? Well, about time. Maybe that explains why he's in such a bad mood!' Natalie said, then changed the subject. She did not want to talk about Sam; she preferred to forget him whenever she could.

Or rather, she would like to; she hadn't yet managed it. However hard she tried not to think about him he kept turning up in her head; it was like being haunted.

Quickly she said, 'Good programme this morning, Johnny; I loved the lady of seventy looking for a new boyfriend. Did she get any calls later?'

Johnny appeared to be running something resembling a radio dating service that week; he kept getting wistful phone calls from people wanting to get some love into their life. If anyone rang in response Johnny would pass on their phone numbers to the original caller, who could then decide whether or not to take it further.

'Thirty old guys rang in to say they would like to meet her,' he said with satisfaction. 'And one weirdo of about twenty who said he really fancied older women.'

Natalie made a face. 'Aren't there some crazy people around?'

'You should hear some of my calls! We never put the really kooky ones on the air!' said Johnny, forking up some of his salad. 'Mmm…this is good, isn't it? I see you got it too—we obviously have a lot in common. Which reminds me, when are we going to have dinner? You keep promising to meet me. How about this weekend? Tomorrow night? We could drive along the coast to a little place I know, have dinner, dance, talk. What do you think?'

She was about to turn him down as nicely as she could, because she knew Johnny was no safer a bet for a woman than Sam, when out of the corner of her eye she realised that Sam was only a couple of tables away from them, drinking coffee with a couple of local businessmen who were at the station that day to buy advertising space on air. Natalie didn't know if he had overheard Johnny's invitation, but as she glanced sideways at him Sam looked back, his grey eyes hard and hostile.

Having him look at her like that made her angry. It was no business of his who she went out with! Who did he think he was? Her father?

Pushed into acting recklessly, she said to Johnny, 'Thanks, I'd love to.'

Are you mad? she asked herself at the very same time. Why are you doing this? You don't want to get involved with Johnny. He's a nice guy, fun to be with, but strictly off-limits for anyone with a single brain cell in her head.

Okay, so Sam glared at you. So what? You're a big girl. You can cope with Sam's glares, can't you? You don't have to be provoked into doing something stupid just to teach Sam a lesson. Then she thought with a thud of the heart, *What lesson? What am I doing? What am I think-ing?*

Johnny leaned over the table and took her hand before she could stop him. Lifting it to his lips in a stagey gesture he murmured huskily, 'That's made my day! I can't wait for tomorrow night. Give me your address and I'll pick you up at around seven, okay?'

Very pink and very conscious of icy eyes observing her, Natalie recovered her hand and hunted in her bag for a pen and the little notepad she carried around with her. She wrote her address down, tore out that page, and handed it to Johnny, who put it into the top pocket of his usual black leather jacket.

All the time the back of Natalie's neck was prickling with nerves. She knew others in the canteen were watch-ing them avidly and listening to every word they could pick up. Some of Johnny's jealous fans among the staff would hate her for getting his attention. But that didn't bother her.

It was just one pair of eyes which were making the hair stand up on her nape. She was instantly aware when Sam got up and walked towards the canteen exit. The table at which she and Johnny sat was not on the direct route to the door, but Sam deviated from the direct route and came past them, halting.

'Enjoying yourselves?' his cold voice enquired, and Natalie made the mistake of looking up into the winter of his stare: icy, distant and hostile.

He was wearing an impressive suit today, for a meet-ing he had had with one of the directors of the company. Natalie felt her mouth dry; the way Sam looked would be wasted on another man. Not on her, though. She had been thinking all morning how intensely sexy Sam looked in the well-cut dark grey suit. The smooth jacket was open at the moment, letting her see the waistcoat tightly clipping his slim waist, the red-striped shirt and dark red silk tie. The way he stood there, confronting them, gave him the look of a matador, psyched up to make a kill.

She hurriedly looked away again, not answering, but Johnny cheerfully said, 'I always enjoy being with Natalie.'

Natalie kept her eyes lowered, fully aware of the way Sam was eying her. What did he mean by looking at her like that?

Curtly he told her, 'We've got a lot to do this afternoon. Don't be late back.' A second later he was gone, the canteen doors swinging noisily behind him, and she could breathe again.

'That is a guy with a serious problem!' Johnny drawled, and as Natalie glanced at him she saw dancing amusement in his eyes.

Suspicion stiffened her spine. What was Johnny up to? Had he asked her out for rather more complex reasons than she had imagined? She could deal with a straightforward pass from him, one arm tied behind her back, but there was a lot more to his invitation than that, it seemed. Was he competing with Sam? Why on earth would he want to? He had girls falling over themselves to get his attention. And what made him think Sam would care if he dated her?

Her blood ran wildly in her veins. Yes. What made him think that? He was crazy. She was crazy, even hoping...

Who's hoping? she asked herself, getting angry again. I know there's no chance... No, that wasn't what I meant. I know Sam isn't interested in me, except as a valuable secretary he doesn't want to lose.

'I'd better get back to work before he pages me on the tannoy,' she said, getting up.

'See you tomorrow,' Johnny said softly, with a flirtatious look.

Natalie's feet slowed once she was out of the canteen—she was in no hurry to face Sam.

She'd been afraid he was going to be in his most difficult mood, would shout or snap at her, but he concentrated on work and barely looked at her, which somehow was worse. It was like talking through a megaphone with a man on a distant mountain peak, which was very disorientating. How did you work with someone who wouldn't look at you and talked in a remote, icy tone all the time?

She didn't know how much more of this she could take. Especially as they were alone together much of the time in a small, confined space. It was like being in a cage with a hungry tiger.

Every so often she would turn round to find herself too close to Sam, would see his intent stare, hear his breathing, and panic would streak through her—although why she should feel so threatened just because Sam looked at her she couldn't say.

On the Friday afternoon she knowingly clockwatched; dying for the moment when she could get away. Sam caught her at it and glared.

'Will you stop looking at that clock? I suppose you've got a date tonight and can't wait for it!'

She glared right back. 'What if I have? Why shouldn't I have a date?'

He took a step nearer than he had all week, she could almost hear him vibrating, poised as if he might lunge for her at any minute. 'Who with? I didn't know you were seeing anyone?'

'I don't tell you everything! You've never asked before—and if you did I wouldn't tell you. I work for you—you don't own me!'

He was so tense she could see the bones pushing through his skin, his face hot with rage.

'That's right—you work for me! So don't talk to me like that again!'

She stood her ground, but she was shaking and couldn't answer him.

'I hope it isn't Linklater you're seeing,' Sam snapped. 'Was that what you two were up to in the canteen yesterday? Were you making a date with him?'

Hoarsely she managed to throw back at him, 'That's my business.'

His grey eyes flashed. 'If it is going to disrupt my working life it's my business, too!'

'Why should it disrupt your life if I have a date with Johnny?'

Sam drew audible breath, staring down at her with confusion in his face as if her question had shaken him, and her heart picked up speed. What did that look mean? It couldn't be...no, Sam would never be jealous over her. Be serious! she told herself—never mind all this wishful thinking. You know Sam. He wouldn't be jealous if you had a whole football team lined up waiting for a date. Whatever is going on here it cannot be personal. Can it? And her bones seemed to melt inside her skin at the very possibility.

'I need you with your head in good working order,' Sam bit out sharply. 'And Johnny Linklater has a well-known effect on women; he addles their brains.'

'He won't addle mine. My brain is fine, thanks, and my private life is my own affair; it has nothing to do with my job. So back off, would you? Mind your own business. Now, can we finish working on this series proposal so that I can get home on time?'

Sam almost said something, she could feel his rage burning the air between them as they stared aggressively at each other, but then he turned his back and went on, brusquely, dictating an answer to the producer who had suggested a new music series for late-night listening. Natalie let a held breath out.

When she left half an hour later she said, 'Have a nice weekend,' from the door.

Sam was hunched over his desk, skimming through a pile of scripts. He looked up, didn't smile, just grunted while his narrowed eyes slid down over her from her dark head to her long legs and small feet.

Natalie didn't know what the grunt was supposed to mean, let alone the slow, almost absent-minded assessment of the way she looked, but she wasn't staying around to find out. She almost ran to the lift and escaped while she could, but she kept thinking about Sam's wandering gaze and suddenly realised it wasn't the first time he had stared at her legs that way. Come to think of it— he often had. She hadn't thought about it before, although she had always been aware of him looking.

Pure male instinct, she had told herself every time he did it. But what sort of instinct? And how pure was it?

Oh, stop trying to kid yourself! she thought. Sam doesn't fancy you; if he did, he would have done something about it long ago. Don't be so pathetic.

As she was walking away from the radio station she saw Helen West's car pulling into the car park. It was a very warm day; the singer had her car top down, the breeze blowing her red hair across her face. She was wearing a brief suntop which showed rather a lot of her—bare arms, her throat, the milky white skin of her breasts and even some of her midriff.

Men walking along the street turned to goggle at her. Helen West gave the quiet English seaside resort the glamour of the Cote d'Azur. Was she on her way to see Sam? Natalie tried to recall whether the singer's name had appeared on any of the day's recording schedules, but she didn't think it had. Helen had a cottage down here, but she spent most of her working life elsewhere— up in London, or touring with the band she usually worked with.

She hadn't been around much this week—was that what had put Sam into a black mood? Maybe Helen had been up in town, and had now come to make up.

Natalie walked on, brooding. Helen West was as real as tinsel, a glittering, sparkling fairy from the top of the Christmas tree—why on earth did men always fall for girls like her?

She got back to her flat at ten to six. The walk home had cleared her head. She was not brooding over Sam any more. She was going to forget him and enjoy herself. He wasn't the only man in the world.

She had plenty of time to have a shower and get dressed in a blue silk dress with a scooped neckline, tight waist and full skirts which fell to mid-calf and swished satisfactorily whenever she moved. Johnny had talked about dancing after dinner, so she had to wear something suitable, and, having only just bought the dress a month or so ago, enchanted when she'd caught sight of it in a shop window in London on a day trip, she had been dying for an opportunity to wear it for the first time.

The colour was so gorgeous: a deep hyacinth which brought out the blue of her eyes and made her skin look creamy. She blowdried her dark hair to a sleek bell shape, took ten minutes to do her make-up, sprayed herself with her favourite French perfume, and was just ready when Johnny arrived dead on seven to pick her up.

For once Johnny wasn't wearing his usual casual gear; he was eye-catching and resplendent in a white evening jacket, stiff white shirt and scarlet bow tie, with a scarlet cummerbund at his waist and black trousers.

'You look marvellous, Johnny!' Natalie said impulsively. One rarely saw him dressed like that and it suited him.

He grinned, pleased by the compliment. 'Thanks. And I've never seen you look so beautiful. Thank you for dressing up for me. I'm honoured.'

She was taken aback by his gravity, especially when he took her hand, lifted it to his lips and kissed it with bowed head.

Oh, dear, she thought—it would be very awkward if Johnny got serious about her. Surely he wouldn't? She had never seen any sign of it before, and it wouldn't just have sprung up overnight like a field mushroom, would it? She knew she could never be serious about Johnny; she liked him, was fond of him, but no way could she ever think of him as anything but a friend.

'I didn't know what colour you were wearing, so I went for white,' he said, bewildering her until he produced a cellophane box from behind his back and handed it to her.

She gazed at the large white magnolia inside, astonished by the sight of it. 'Oh, Johnny, how beautiful—is it real?' It was the sort of extravagant gesture he was famous for, but she had never been on the receiving end before.

'Flown in from the States overnight, the florist told me!'

'All that way? Heavens. I've never seen a magnolia

in a florist's, only growing on trees in a garden! Billie Holiday used to wear them, didn't she? How long will it last?' The waxen petals looked as if a fingertip touch might bruise and discolour the pure whiteness.

'It will last the night.' Johnny shrugged. 'Let me pin it on for you!'

He opened the box and got out the magnolia, gave it to her, then coolly took hold of the scalloped neckline of her dress, between finger and thumb, and carefully pinned the flower just above her left breast, making Natalie feel faintly shy. But Johnny didn't say or do anything to alarm her; the flower in place, he stepped back and admired the effect.

'Perfect with that blue—I couldn't have chosen anything better.'

Natalie turned away from him to consider her own reflection in the mirror hanging by her front door, and had to agree. The enormous cup-like flower glowed, brilliant white, against the hyacinth-blue silk.

'Thank you, Johnny, it's gorgeous!'

'So are you,' he said, and again Natalie felt a twinge of unease—what was going on here? Why was Johnny paying her these extravagant compliments?

'I don't want to hurry you, but I've booked dinner at eight, and it will take me nearly an hour to drive along the coast, Natalie. So, if you're ready, could we leave now?'

It was a magical evening for a drive; the air was like warm wine and they had the windows right down as they drove, to allow a little breeze to blow some coolness across their faces. Leaning out of her window, Natalie watched black-headed gulls flying over the halcyon waves and a little flock of ringed plovers feeding on the edge of the sea, their bright orange legs very visible as they ran along, heads lowered in search of molluscs, insects and worms. Shadows were lengthening over the cliffs, but night at this time of the year descended so slowly that it was still very light when they reached the hotel where Johnny had booked a table for dinner.

They were greeted obsequiously by the head waiter, who recognised Johnny the instant they walked in and showed them at once to a table beside a window overlooking the sea. There were carnations and roses in a low bowl in the centre of the table, their scent still strong. While they chose from the large menu they sipped champagne cocktails and listened to the small band playing popular songs on the dais at the end of the ballroom opening out of the dining room.

On such a warm evening Natalie wanted something light and cool, so she chose melon filled with summer berries followed by cold poached salmon with minted new potatoes and salad. Johnny had the melon, too, but filled with hot prawns in a mild chilli sauce, and then a steak, in a red wine and mushroom sauce.

They took ages to eat, talking all the time, mostly about Johnny's career so far and his plans for the future. But from time to time he asked her casual questions which she soon realised were actually very serious, questions worrying him, and possibly the real reason why Johnny had asked her out.

He was terrified of losing his niche at the station, terrified of losing his audience, of his ratings dropping. He knew very well that his shelf-life was finite, and that Sam held the key. Sam had the power of life and death for Johnny. Was that why he had asked Natalie out? Was he hoping to use her to influence Sam? It was Sam he seemed really interested in—he kept asking her what Sam's plans were for the year ahead, whether Sam intended to stay at the radio station or move on to something bigger and more important, if Sam had any new ideas for music programmes, what Sam's opinions were on other disc jockeys, other music and chat shows.

Natalie answered discreetly, without giving anything much away, watching him across the table in the soft lamplight. At such close quarters that tanned face was not as young-looking as it seemed at a distance. There were fine lines around eyes and mouth, not to mention a faint puffiness under the eyes and hollows in his throat. In a few years Johnny would look middle-aged; he couldn't hold time at bay much longer and she felt a surge of sympathy for him.

True, radio was not as unforgiving as television, and, true, the listeners rarely saw him in the flesh. The signed photos he sent out were a few years old, and carefully touched up to hide his age. But for how much longer could he pull in a teenage audience? He might hold onto the older listeners for a few more years, but Johnny's glory days were over. No wonder he was terrified.

When they had spent half an hour over coffee they went through into the ballroom, and a buzz of excitement ran through the room. As usual, female eyes were glued on Johnny, who, of course, knew it, and took on a new lease of life, his eyes very bright under that lime-light.

A table had been reserved for them on the edge of the dance floor. The wine waiter came over at once, but as Johnny was driving he was on sparkling mineral water from now on; he had drunk very little champagne over dinner.

They danced for a while, which would have been pleasant—Natalie loved the way her dark blue silk skirts swung around her as she moved—but she felt self-conscious with all those eyes on her. She wasn't used to being watched like that.

When they sat down again a couple came over to their

table, grinning at Johnny. 'Hi, Johnny—how are you?' said the young man, who was wearing a vivid orange jacket and lime-green shirt—colours which clashed horribly, in Natalie's opinion, especially when worn with lime-green cotton trousers and a lime-green striped tie. She had never seen an outfit like it, in fact. The owner had big, bright green eyes and a mop of curly brown hair. Natalie had a feeling she knew him—but couldn't place the face.

Until Johnny said, 'Hey, Spider! Great to see you again. That new disc of yours is ace, man. Been playing it all week.'

His name and face clicked, then, in Natalie's memory—Spider Rex was one of the latest crop of singers they were playing on air. He was in his early twenties, but looked years younger.

'Hey, thanks, man,' Spider said.

His companion, a much younger girl, with outrageously dyed orange-blonde hair, which almost matched Spider's jacket, and wearing a very tight sparkly pink shift in which she could only just walk on her very high pink heels, dug her elbow into Spider's ribs. He looked round and she made a pouting gesture to Johnny.

Drily, Spider said, 'Johnny, this is my girlfriend, Cindy. Cindy, Johnny.'

Johnny smiled his heartbreaking smile at her and the girl put her arm round his neck and kissed him full on the mouth.

Spider did not look happy about this.

She's stoned! thought Natalie, seeing the dark, wet shine of the girl's pupils. The slender body under the tinsel-like dress appeared boneless; she hung onto Johnny as if to keep herself from falling down.

'Dance?' Cindy breathed sultrily.

'Okay, babe,' Johnny said, then with an obvious effort

dragged his eyes away from her to look at Spider, his expression wary. 'That okay with you, Spidey?'

Spider shrugged, face sulky. 'Take her, if you want her. She's too high to make sense.'

'High?' repeated Johnny. 'What's she on? Nothing disastrous, I hope? We don't want any trouble.'

Cindy didn't even wait for Spider to answer. Her arm still crooked round Johnny's neck, she dragged him onto the parquet floor and began to dance, moving around him with a bright, mad smile.

Spider stood watching them, his body stiff with insult. For a moment it looked as if he was going to walk off, then he seemed to remember Natalie. He looked at her assessingly. 'Wanna dance?'

'Very kind of you, but I think I'll leave,' Natalie said, getting up. 'Goodnight. Tell Johnny I'm taking a taxi home.'

Spider followed her and caught hold of her elbow. 'I'll drive you home. I'm going, too.'

They had almost reached the exit when Cindy became aware that they were leaving. She stopped dancing and came tottering after them on her stilt-like heels, yelling, 'Spider! Hey, where are you going?'

'Get lost!' He pushed her away.

'Oh, I get it—she picked you up!' Cindy hissed like a snake and lunged, but not at Spider—her fury was turned on Natalie. As she went for Natalie's face with her long, pointy scarlet nails she started calling her names that made Natalie's hair curl. Instinctively she shoved the other girl away, and at that moment Johnny intervened to grab Natalie while Spider caught Cindy by the waist and lifted her up in the air, kicking and struggling.

At that second a flash of lightning made Natalie jump. Then she realised in horror that it wasn't lightning; it was flashbulbs popping. Oh, no, not the Press! she thought, covering her face with her arm.

'Let's get out of here,' Johnny said, taking her wrist.

They ran for the exit, leaving Spider and Cindy fighting while flashbulbs exploded all round them.

Out in the cool night air Johnny groaned. 'That was bad luck! I had no idea there was a photographer around.' He looked down at her. 'You okay? I'm sorry to have got you into that, Natalie. Come on, I'll drive you home.'

She was inclined to refuse, she was angry with him for going off to dance with the other girl, but she didn't want to go back into the hotel to ask them to phone for a taxi, and it would cost the earth to get a taxi from here anyway, so she followed him across the car park.

They didn't talk much while they drove home; Johnny was playing tapes all the way and Natalie was sleepy. She stared out of the car window at the heaving, glittering sea with moonlight drifting over it. Melancholy possessed her. It was a very romantic night. The music was romantic, too.

Why was she with the wrong man?

CHAPTER FIVE

NATALIE woke up late the next morning. As her eyes opened to broad sunlight she automatically rolled over to look at the clock, forgetting that this was Saturday and she didn't have to go to work, saw that it was gone ten, groaned and sat bolt-upright. It took another second or two for her to remember what day it was and to sink back against her pillows, closing her eyes again, remembering last night.

A pity about that scene at the end. Biting her lower lip, she hoped none of the national papers got hold of those photos. Sam would be furious. He had warned her not to date Johnny, but how in the world could she ever have guessed anything like that would happen? Not that Sam was likely to accept that as an excuse. He could be very unreasonable when he was in a temper, and lately he was always in a temper.

She couldn't get back to sleep once she had begun thinking about Sam, so she got up, showered, and got dressed in blue denim jeans and a white T-shirt. Then she had a late breakfast of coffee and orange juice and some strawberries she had bought yesterday. They were delicious with yoghurt.

Saturday mornings were always devoted to housework. She spent an hour tidying her flat and cleaning it: vacuuming, dusting, polishing, sorting out her washing and putting it on, and bundling up the week's newspapers to take to the paper recycling bin which stood in the supermarket car park a short drive away.

Her shopping only took a few minutes; she disposed

of her old newspapers, bottles and cans in the appropriate containers and then drove back home to put her shopping away before she left for Mrs Erskine's cottage. The
phone was ringing as she put her key in the lock, but by
the time she got inside the ringing had stopped. She left
again within minutes.

It was another gorgeous day, the sky a glowing, halcyon blue, the sea calm, the temperature building up by
noon into what promised to be an almost tropical heatwave. In the back of the car she had her easel and art
equipment; she had brought a big, floppy straw hat, too,
to provide some shade while she painted. She had
bought the hat in Spain a couple of years ago and had
rarely had an opportunity to wear it since, as English
summers were not often very hot.

Mrs Erskine lived on the downs, half an hour's drive
away. Her village, Abbotslea, was so small that if you
drove too fast you didn't even notice it. A ribbon development of little cottages along the road, a big
Victorian church, an old black and white timbered pub,
and you were out of the village again. Mrs Erskine's
cottage was not on the main road, though, it stood alone,
in a big garden, on a little road leading up onto the
downs.

Natalie parked her little car on the driveway, put on
her hat, got out her painting equipment and walked up
to the front door, breathing in the heavy scent of honeysuckle which grew in profusion up the wall of the cottage, twisting and sprawling, thick with creamy orange
flowers whose fragrance met you at the gate. The front
garden had a smoothly mown lawn around which grew
towering dark blue spikes of delphiniums and great
blood-red glowing globes of peony, white arum lilies
with golden throats and roses, whose perfume in the sun
was almost as powerful as that of the honeysuckle.

Around the front door stood an old green trellis porch in which the honeysuckle twined with climbing yellow roses. Before Natalie could knock, the front door opened and Mrs Erskine smiled a welcome.

'Hello, Natalie. Isn't it a lovely day? How wise of you to bring a hat; you could get sunstroke painting outside today. Come in and put your painting gear out on the patio while I pour you a drink—what would you like? Some white wine? Orange or apple juice? Mineral water?'

'Apple juice would be marvellous, thank you.'

Natalie followed her into the cool interior, looking about her. A small hall gave way to a larger kitchen, down a couple of steps. The floors were stone flags, sunk with age, gleaming with the polish of years, and ridged straw mats were spread here and there.

The kitchen itself was painted yellow, with a well-used Aga stove in a recess, a large oak dresser full of china and glass along one wall, and one small window beside that, looking out onto the garden with a row of geraniums in terracotta pots standing on the window-ledge. There was a tall glass door standing open at the far end of the room, leading out onto a patio beyond which Natalie glimpsed more garden, grass and trees, stretching off into the distance with the green swell of the downs beyond that.

She carried her painting gear out onto the patio and then stood there gazing out into the blue horizon, which glittered and shimmered with heat. There was no other house in sight and the only sounds were natural ones—the rustle of leaves, birds calling, the constant murmur of the sea.

'Here you are, my dear,' Mrs Erskine said, handing her a tall, frosted glass of apple juice with leaves of mint and crushed ice bobbing up and down on top of it. 'Lunch is ready; I'll bring it out here.'

'Let me help you.' Natalie put her glass down on a table which was already laid for two and stood under a white sun umbrella whose fringe danced and fluttered in a little breeze.

'No need. Everything is ready on a trolley. I'll just wheel it out. You sit down at the table.'

Mrs Erskine walked back into the house, and returned at once, pushing a trolley. Natalie helped her move a large bowl of salad onto the centre of the table, then an earthenware dish of rice, cooked with peas, fine trails of fried onion, sweetcorn and red pepper, a basket of wholemeal rolls, a large bottle of mineral water standing in an ice bucket and finally a hot, cooked chicken which had a delicious aroma.

'What a marvellous smell—what did you cook it in?' Natalie asked, accepting some chicken and inhaling more of the mouthwatering scent.

'Honey and mustard and brown sugar. Help yourself to salad, rice and a roll, Natalie. I made these myself— they rose quite well. My wholemeal bread doesn't always rise; I'm told I don't knead it well enough.'

'My mother says she always makes bread whenever she's in a real temper; the kneading helps to use up her aggression.'

'Oh, I do agree. When I want to hit someone I often make some bread.'

'Pity I can't do that in the office when Sam's in one of his moods!' Natalie sighed, then caught Sam's mother's eye and went pink. 'Oh, sorry. I didn't mean...'

'I know how maddening he can be—none better!' Mrs Erskine said. 'He was a horrible little boy.'

'I can imagine,' Natalie said, smiling. The very idea of Sam as a little boy made her feel weak inside. How stupid! she thought. Are you out of your mind? He isn't a little boy any more. He's a great big horrible man and you are asking for trouble letting yourself moon over him like this. Where's your common sense?

Yet she couldn't stop herself asking, 'What was he like when he was small?'

'I'll show you some photos later,' his mother said. 'Have you always painted, Natalie?'

'Ever since I picked up my first crayon, so my mother says. I drew a circle on the wall of my bedroom, and got smacked for it.'

'Giotto was famous for being able to draw a perfect circle while he was still a small child.'

'Oh, my circle was far from perfect— it was meant to be a face. I put two dots in the middle of it, but no nose or mouth.'

They went on talking freely and easily while they ate, covering a lot of ground: from how to cook rice to how to mix paints, and from art to radio, which brought in Sam again, and how he had gone into radio as a trainee, after leaving college, and how exciting he still found working in radio.

Realising that anything about Sam obviously fascinated her to the point of obsession, Natalie hurriedly changed the subject, afraid his mother would guess how she felt; mothers had powerful antennae where their sons were concerned.

'What did you do before you got married?' she asked.

'I met my husband at college. We got married while we were there, so we lived on bread and cheese for a couple of years until Jack joined the army and began earning enough for us to have a baby.'

'Sam,' Natalie thought aloud, unable to stop herself. There I go again! For pity's sake, can't I keep that man out of my head?

His mother smiled at her and Natalie hoped it wasn't an indulgent pitying smile. She hoped Mrs Erskine hadn't caught on to how she felt about Sam. She must try not to be so obvious.

'Sam,' Mrs Erskine agreed. 'Life in the army means moving around all the time, and wherever Jack went I was determined to go, too, so for a few years we didn't have any more children. I felt I had enough to do just looking after Sam and packing and unpacking every few months. When Jack left the army and we settled down in Scotland, though, I had my two girls—which is why there's a big gap between Sam and his sisters.'

Her face saddened and she sighed. 'When Sam was sixteen, my husband was killed, climbing in the Himalayas. He was very much an outdoor man, never happier than when he was risking his life. Sam has inherited a lot of his father's character, but not that particular gene, thank God. He learnt young that if you chuck your life away you can hurt the people you care about. He was devastated when his father died. After that he tried to step into his father's shoes; he saw himself as the man of the family and tried to take care of me and his sisters. They adored him, of course; he was so much older than them, and had a lot of glamour. And then Jeanie turned fifteen and stopped being a little girl and started wanting to be a woman.'

Natalie smiled, remembering herself at that age. 'As we all do!'

'Of course. Those are difficult years, even when you're rebelling against your father, but when the rules are being laid down by your big brother... Well, it isn't surprising that Jeanie started yelling at him every time he opened his mouth, but Sam wasn't her father, or old enough to understand what she was going through. He just lost his temper and told her to do what she was told, or else!'

'Sounds familiar. I've always wondered why Sam is such a tyrant. Now I know! He's had years of ordering people about. He seems to get on well with Jeanie and Marie now, though.'

'Most of the time.' His mother nodded. 'If he starts laying down the law, though, the girls turn round and tell him where he can jump.'

'I'd like to see that,' Natalie said wistfully. She met Mrs Erskine's eyes again, and they both laughed.

They drank some coffee before clearing the table together, reloading the trolley and wheeling it back into the house. Natalie insisted on helping to put all the plates, cutlery and cooking dishes into the dishwasher, then they covered the rest of the chicken, rice and salad with clingfilm and put it away in the fridge. After that, Mrs Erskine showed her the downstairs cloakroom, where she washed her face and hands, renewed her make-up and brushed her hair.

They began to paint at two o'clock; the sun was high, there was almost no breeze at all by then, and the shadows of trees lay in black, unmoving pools on the grass. Her hat on her head, keeping the sun off her face, Natalie worked slowly and thoughtfully on a watercolour of a big sycamore tree, with a cluster of holly trees in front of it and deep pink foxgloves growing beyond, while in the distance she painted the blue sea, the blue sky, and a little flock of white gulls between them.

'May I look at what you've done, or don't you like anyone to see it until it's finished?' Mrs Erskine said, appearing at her side.

Natalie gestured. 'It's almost finished now—what do you think? That tree looks a bit shaky, doesn't it?'

Mrs Erskine stood beside her, looked for a long time,

then said, 'You know, you're really very good, aren't you? Why didn't you take it up professionally?'

Natalie grimaced. 'I'm not good enough—just a Sunday painter, I'm afraid. But I'd rather be a good Sunday painter than a bad professional.'

'Well, I love this picture—I suppose you wouldn't let me buy it? I'm always painting this view but I never manage to paint it as well as that.'

'When I've finished it, and had it framed, I'll give it to you as a thank-you for my lunch! It was one of the best meals I've ever eaten. It's a fair swap!'

Mrs Erskine flushed with pleasure. 'Thank you, my dear.'

'May I look at your painting, too?'

'Of course—but I warn you, it isn't as good as yours. I don't have your touch with a brush.'

Natalie could see why when she looked at the picture—Mrs Erskine's use of colour was slightly muddy; greens and blues and browns ran into each other and blurred the images she tried to paint.

'What do you think I'm doing wrong?' Mrs Erskine asked.

'Well...' Natalie was reluctant to proffer advice; people sometimes asked for it then resented what you said.

'Be frank, Natalie! You won't upset me.'

Slowly Natalie said, 'Well, I think the reason why you don't get the sharpness of outline you need might be that you paint too fast and try to get it all down at once. When you had painted that tree, for instance, you should have let it dry before starting on the foxgloves; that's why you've got the only foxgloves in the world with greeny pink petals.'

Mrs Erskine laughed loudly. 'I saw that happen! You're absolutely right, of course. When I first began painting, I would put a picture aside to dry before completing it...but I ended up with so many half-finished pictures that I stopped bothering, and now I just rush to finish it in a day.' She yawned. 'It's so hot I'm half-asleep. Would you think I was very rude if I went and had a siesta for an hour while you're finishing your picture? Then we can have tea when I wake up, and I'll show you those photos of Sam as a baby.'

Natalie felt her skin glow with heat. 'Don't worry about me; I'll be perfectly happy. I haven't much left to paint.'

Mrs Erskine studied her hot face shrewdly. 'You look hot, my dear. When you've finished, have a dip in the stream. It's over there, behind the hedge; it isn't very deep but the water is pure—it comes from the downs, filtered through chalk, and there is nothing here to pollute it. On really hot days like this the children always used to swim in it. Wait here on the patio and I'll throw you down a towel and one of Jeanie's swimsuits—it will fit you; you're about the same size as her.'

Startled, Natalie said, 'Are you sure she won't mind?'

'Absolutely certain. She has half a dozen.'

'Well, thank you—that's a tempting idea. I am very hot.'

Mrs Erskine went into the house and a few minutes later called Natalie from a window upstairs. She threw down a large green towel with a swimsuit wrapped inside it, gave her a wave and vanished again.

Natalie painted on for another ten minutes, until she was satisfied with her picture, then she went into the house, found the downstairs cloakroom again and changed into Jeanie's neat black swimsuit, which fitted her just slightly too tightly.

She walked down towards the hedge running along one side of the garden, her towel under her arm, but had only gone a little way when she heard footsteps inside the house.

She turned to listen, frowning. Was that Mrs Erskine? Whoever it was was moving very carefully and quietly. Natalie hesitated, then tiptoed back to the house, put her towel down on the patio table and softly crept to the open kitchen door.

She couldn't see anyone, but she could still hear furtive movements somewhere. A heavy wooden rolling pin hung on the kitchen wall; Natalie silently detached it from its hook, held it tightly and moved out into the hall.

A man stood there with his back to her. In the cool shadows of the hall she couldn't make out much about him except that he was worryingly tall and well built, and wearing jeans with something black over them. But she saw him pick up a silver-framed photograph and knew she had been right. He was a burglar.

'Oh, no, you don't! Put that back and get out of here!' Natalie shouted. 'I've got a weapon here and I'll use it if I have to.'

The tall figure stiffened.

'Put that photograph back!' Natalie repeated.

He coolly replaced it on the mantelpiece from which he had taken it, then pivoted and took a step towards her.

Natalie instinctively lifted her rolling pin, poised to jump at him. 'Don't come any closer! Just go, if you don't want your head smashed in!'

He took another step closer and light fell on his face. Natalie sagged, groaning.

'Sam! What on earth were you doing, creeping about like that? I thought you were a burglar.'

'I was trying not to wake my mother up! She always

has a rest at this time of the afternoon. And stop waving that rolling pin at me. You're making me nervous.'

He took it out of her hand and went into the kitchen to hang it back in its original place. Natalie followed him, her throat beating with awareness.

Sam swung round and looked at her, his grey eyes widening as he noticed for the first time that she was only wearing a swimsuit. He stared at her long, bare legs, then upwards, slowly, over her smooth hips, the small waist, the half-bare breasts, exploring so hard she felt almost sick.

'I...I was just going for a swim...' she stammered, feeling she had to break the silence, and Sam watched her mouth as she spoke.

'So I see,' he huskily murmured, and the timbre of his voice made her stomach plunge. Then he suddenly frowned and his face changed, hardened, tightened. Reaching into a pocket in his black cotton shirt, he pulled out a folded piece of paper, shook it out and held it up so that she could see it.

It took a few seconds for Natalie to realise it was a page from a newspaper.

'Have you seen this?' Sam grated through his teeth.

'What is it?'

He pushed it at her and she took it gingerly, drawing a sharp breath as she saw her own face staring up at her. A big photograph headed the column of newsprint. She knew at once what it was—the picture which had been taken last night, in the hotel ballroom. Seen like this, in the cold light of day, it looked far worse than she remembered it. Johnny held her by the waist, his hands just below her breasts, and she was staring in open-eyed, open-mouthed shock into the camera, looking dazed, as if she might be as stoned as Cindy had been.

The picture showed the pop singer, Spider, too, carrying a struggling, kicking Cindy, who for some odd reason didn't look stoned at all. She'd been too angry; she looked half-crazy.

Hurriedly lowering the paper, Natalie nervously said, 'It looks worse than it was!'

'You didn't read the story!'

Reluctantly she looked back at the page, wincing as her eyes moved down the print, very conscious of Sam scowling beside her.

'Thank heavens they didn't get my name!' she said, slowly looking back at him and feeling the hairs on the back of her neck stand up at his expression. Why was Sam so furious? It was hardly a hanging offence, getting her picture in the paper, especially as they hadn't named her.

'You see what they called you?' he icily asked her. ''Johnny Linklater's latest babe''!'

It sounded so comic she laughed before she had known she was going to, and Sam's eyes flashed. 'Oh, you think that's funny? You like being called a babe?'

'Of course not. I just...'

Sam's mouth twisted cynically. 'Oh, don't deny it. I suppose you're flattered, being linked publicly with Linklater? You think the paper makes you sound like a teenager? I know half the female staff are always sighing over him, although God knows why, but then women have a weird idea of what's sexy.'

'If women didn't find him sexy they wouldn't listen to his show, and you wouldn't bother to put it out!' Natalie eyed him scornfully. 'You want it all ways, don't you? You run Johnny down, yet you're only too happy to broadcast his show. You know what they call that, don't you? Hypocrisy.'

Sam stiffened, his black brows level and angry. 'No, they call it the radio business,' he bit out. 'I run the station to make money, and Linklater's show attracts a lot of listeners and therefore a lot of advertisers. My personal view of him has nothing to do with business.'

She was very angry now. 'But you just love to sit in judgement on him! And on me, too. But you of all people have no right to take the moral high ground. And who I date has nothing to do with you.'

He looked at her furiously. 'Don't tell me you enjoyed that sordid little scene?'

Natalie defiantly tried to hold his stare, but couldn't because he was right—she had hated what happened. Looking away, she dropped the newspaper onto the kitchen table, wishing she dared risk chucking it at him. She was just in a mood to throw something at Sam, but she was afraid of what he might do in return.

'It wasn't Johnny's fault,' she defended. 'It was Cindy—this girl Spider had with him. She made Johnny dance with her, so I decided to go home, and Spider said he would drive me. But she came after us and made a jealous scene. Everything would have been okay if a photographer hadn't happened to be there.'

Ignoring all that, Sam drily repeated, 'She *made* Johnny dance with her? How did she do that? Pull a gun on him?'

Natalie gave him a furious, resentful look. 'She grabbed him and dragged him on the floor, actually!'

'And he fought every inch of the way, of course!'

'Okay, she was a sexy little brat—one of those teenagers Johnny always fancies, a sort of living doll. Men do like the sparkly dollies of this world, don't they? You should know that.'

He held her gaze, his eyes narrowed. 'You think I like that sort of girl?'

'Judging by past company, yes.'

'Now who is taking the moral high ground? You don't approve of the sort of girl I date?'

'None of my business,' she muttered, head bent. If he wanted to go out with girls like Helen West why should she care? 'I'm going for my swim!' She sidled towards the door onto the patio but didn't get very far.

'I haven't finished with you!' Sam's long fingers grabbed her by the shoulders.

His touch made her body burn and she couldn't hide her reaction. Face hot, she breathed raggedly, not able to meet his eyes, not even able to get a word out, to protest or tell him to let her go.

She felt him watching her, felt, too, the warmth of his fingertips on her bare skin, almost believed she could feel his heart beating where he touched her, as if the blood pulsing through his veins carried the sound of that heartbeat to his fingertips and transferred it through her skin so that her own heart began to beat in harmony with his.

'What's the matter, Natalie?' Sam said in a low, husky voice. 'Why are you so agitated all of a sudden?'

She swallowed. 'I don't like being manhandled!' The lie was pathetic but she had to say something, didn't she? She couldn't tell him the truth—couldn't say, Just having you touch me is making my bones melt and my heart crash about inside my chest like a ship lost on rocks, because I think I'm in love with you, but I'd rather die than let you guess.

'Is that all?' Was it her imagination, or did Sam sound as if he didn't believe her? What had he thought she would say, for heaven's sake? Did he know...or guess...or suspect...how she felt? She closed her eyes, stricken with horror at the very idea of Sam being aware of her stupid, unwanted, pointless, hopeless emotions. She was behaving like a schoolgirl with a crush. Oh,

God, what would he think if he did guess? He would probably be sorry for her, and that would be the deepest circle of hell. She wanted to sink down through the floor and never be seen again at the very thought of Sam pitying her for loving him.

'Let go of me,' she whispered, and Sam's fingers relaxed their grip on her shoulders. But he didn't let go. Instead his fingers slid very slowly, very softly, down her bare arms, raising goosebumps everywhere they touched, until they got to her wrists. There they locked, iron bracelets holding her prisoner.

'Don't!' she broke out, looking up angrily, and a second later was jerked forward.

She couldn't stop herself; her body hit his, knocking all the breath out of her, not so much from the force of the contact as from the contact itself, from feeling his body against hers, touching her, his chest, his midriff, his thigh. She was aware of every inch of him. She shook violently, couldn't stop the tremors running through her from head to foot, couldn't stop her knees giving.

Especially when Sam leaned even closer, put his cheek against hers so that she felt his long, silky lashes brushing her skin.

His mouth against her ear, he whispered, 'Why are you trembling, Natalie? Why is your face so flushed?'

She wanted to turn her face and find his mouth, but she wouldn't give in to her stupid feelings so she muttered, 'Leave me alone, Sam. I'm not interested. Go and find some other female to play with.'

'Maybe I want to play with you.' He slid his cheek down against hers, turned slightly so that his lips brushed her neck, her bare shoulder, and she couldn't breathe, she was shaking so hard.

'Lovely skin you've got,' Sam said. 'And gorgeous

legs—I can't stop looking at them. I like your perfume; I always have. It fills the air in my office when you've gone and keeps reminding me of you. Sometimes I wake up at night and think I can smell it, which can be very disconcerting.'

Her heart thudded wildly. He was lying, of course; how many other girls had he said these things to? She wasn't going to let him fool her.

'Oh, shut up!' she angrily said. 'Or I'll yell like mad and bring your mother down here to find out what's going on.'

'Go on then!' he silkily dared her, laughing openly.

He didn't believe she would. Natalie opened her mouth to scream, but was too slow. Sam's mouth clamped over hers before she could let out so much as a whimper, and she was lost. Her mouth clung to his, a fierce aching in the pit of her stomach. Sam let go of her hands and pulled her even closer, their bodies straining together. His hands moved down her back, caressed her hips, her naked thighs. Feverishly she clasped his nape and stroked the thick black hair that clung to her fingers, felt the strong muscles under her fingertips, ran a hand down his powerful back, pressing him even nearer.

He slid a hand upwards again, pulled down the strap of her swimsuit, unpeeling the black material from her hot skin, and she caught her breath as he bent his head and kissed her breast, his mouth warmly moist around her nipple.

'Sam…' she groaned, half fainting with pleasure, and he lifted his head to look down at her with half-closed eyes, breathing thickly.

Natalie looked back at him drowsily, almost bewildered by the desire surging through her. Did he feel like this? His skin was as darkly flushed as her own, and as hot; she felt the heat in his body coming off him in waves, and realised how little she knew about men and their feelings. How strange that she had never even thought about it before, never wondered if men's feelings mirrored those of women, or were very different.

His voice sounded strange, unfamiliar. 'I can't believe it took me so long to do that. I'd got so used to seeing you around every day, I didn't really look closely until the other day—although I remember thinking what great legs you had a few times. Now I can't stop thinking about you. I've had you on my mind all week.'

So that was what had been on his mind. She had just thought he was in a temper.

'Ever since that damned party of Johnny's,' he went on. 'Or did it start when I kissed you in the office next morning?' He sounded as if he was talking to himself, thinking aloud. 'Yes, that was it, I think. That kiss changed everything. You felt so good in my arms. I started wondering what you were like in bed, and once I had that in my head I couldn't stop thinking about it. I knew I had to find out. It's got worse every day.'

She listened, the heat draining out of her, feeling suddenly cold.

'I want you, Natalie,' he said urgently, staring down into her eyes as if he was trying to hypnotise her—and maybe that was what he was doing, trying to brainwash her into doing what he wanted. 'I've got to have you. Now. And I can't wait.' He bent and kissed her very hard, very briefly. 'Go and change. I'll drive you home, to my place. We can't risk it here—my mother might come down any minute.'

She wanted to burst into tears, to scream, hit him, but she wasn't a child any more and she had been conditioned by every day of her life not to give way to her deepest instincts. A woman couldn't afford to show her feelings, couldn't admit to any hurt she suffered. So she just went on staring at him as if she was deaf or half-witted, and didn't understand what he was saying.

She understood though, knew that they had been coming from very different places just now. She had been crazy with love for him, but Sam wasn't talking about love. He didn't love her. Love didn't come into it for him. He wanted her, wanted to know what she was like in bed. He said he had to have her. Now. He couldn't wait.

Sam had said he hadn't noticed her before—the truth was, he still hadn't noticed her. He had never even seen her, seen the woman she was, realised how she felt. She was just a body Sam suddenly fancied, and when he had had her no doubt he would walk away, the way he had from all the others before her.

She had been silent so long that Sam's face started to change. 'Natalie?' he said, sounding wary. Maybe she looked as odd as she felt. Maybe he could see madness and rage in her eyes. She knew they must be there.

He hadn't asked her how she felt about him. He didn't care, so long as she didn't make a scene or ask for anything Sam didn't want to give—like love. He had no idea what she was like, what she thought, what tidal waves of desire and passion beat on the shores of her body, what tenderness and caring she could give him.

Sam wanted sex, not tenderness, though, and that was something Natalie wasn't offering.

'Natalie, what's wrong?' he asked, and now there was impatience in his voice. He was in a hurry to get her back to his place, get her into bed. He reached for her again, thinking he hadn't softened her up enough, he had moved too fast. 'Natalie, we don't have time to waste. My mother will be down soon; we have to get going,'

GET FREE BOOKS AND A WONDERFUL FREE GIFT!

TRY YOUR LUCK AT OUR CASINO, WHERE ALL THE GAMES ARE ON THE HOUSE!

PLAY **Roulette!**

PLAY **TWENTY-ONE**

Turn the page and deal yourself in!

Welcome to the casino!
Try your luck at the roulette wheel ...
Play a hand of Twenty-One!

HOW TO PLAY:

1. Play the Roulette and Twenty-One scratch-off games, as instructed on the opposite page, to see if you are eligible for FREE BOOKS and a FREE GIFT!

2. Send back the card and you'll receive TWO brand-new Harlequin Presents® novels. These books have a cover price of $3.75 each, but they are yours to keep absolutely free.

3. There's no catch. You're under no obligation to buy anything. We charge nothing — ZERO — for your first shipment. And you don't have to make any minimum number of purchases — not even one!

4. The fact is, thousands of readers enjoy receiving books by mail from the Harlequin Reader Service® before they're available in stores. They like the convenience of home delivery, and they love our discount prices!

5. We hope that after receiving your free books you'll want to remain a subscriber. But the choice is yours — to continue or cancel, any time at all! So why not take us up on our invitation, with no risk of any kind. You'll be glad you did!

PLAY TWENTY-ONE FOR THIS EXQUISITE FREE GIFT!

THIS SURPRISE MYSTERY GIFT COULD BE YOURS FREE WHEN YOU PLAY

TWENTY-ONE!

It's fun, and we're giving away FREE GIFTS to all players!

PLAY Roulette!

Scratch the silver to see where the ball has landed—7 RED or 11 BLACK makes you eligible for TWO FREE romance novels!

PLAY TWENTY-ONE!

Scratch the silver to reveal a winning hand! Congratulations, you have Twenty-One. Return this card promptly and you'll receive a fabulous free mystery gift, along with your free books!

YES! Please send me all the free Harlequin Presents® books and the gift for which I qualify! I understand that I am under no obligation to purchase any books, as explained on the back of this card.

Name (please print clearly)

Address   Apt.#

City   State   Zip

Offer limited to one per household and not valid to current Harlequin Presents® subscribers. All orders subject to approval.   PRINTED IN U.S.A.

(U-H-P-02/98)   **106 HDL CE5W**

The Harlequin Reader Service® — Here's how it works:

Accepting free books places you under no obligation to buy anything. You may keep the books and gift and return the shipping statement marked "cancel." If you do not cancel, about a month later we'll send you 6 additional novels and bill you just $3.12 each plus 25¢ delivery per book and applicable sales tax, if any.* That's the complete price — and compared to cover prices of $3.75 each — quite a bargain indeed! You may cancel at any time, but if you choose to continue, every month we'll send you 6 more books, which you may either purchase at the discount price...or return to us and cancel your subscription.

*Terms and prices subject to change without notice. Sales tax applicable in N.Y.

If offer card is missing write to: Harlequin Reader Service, 3010 Walden Ave., P.O. Box 1867, Buffalo, NY 14240-9952

BUSINESS REPLY MAIL

FIRST-CLASS MAIL   PERMIT NO 717   BUFFALO NY

POSTAGE WILL BE PAID BY ADDRESSEE

HARLEQUIN READER SERVICE
3010 WALDEN AVE
PO BOX 1867
BUFFALO NY 14240-9952

NO POSTAGE
NECESSARY
IF MAILED
IN THE
UNITED STATES

he whispered, bending to kiss her neck again. But she shoved him away. Hard.

'No,' she got out, her mouth as dry as ashes. Her heart felt like ashes, too, it felt like a dying star, consuming itself, imploding and leaving just a black hole in the loneliness of space. This must be how death felt. She couldn't even cry, she was so desolate.

'What do you mean, no?' Sam was usually so quick, his mind sharp as a razor, but not at the moment. Desire was like a brake on him; he couldn't concentrate on anything but what he wanted. 'You want me, I know you do—do you think I couldn't feel that, just now?'

'You know nothing at all about me, Sam, least of all what I feel and what I want.' She looked into his eyes with bitterness. 'You're so obsessed with yourself you can't even see other people, let alone sense how they feel.'

His face stiffened as if she had hit him. He opened his mouth as if to say something, but she went on hurriedly before he got a word out.

'I wouldn't sleep with you if you were the last man alive, Sam. I like to be able to respect myself, and I wouldn't if I let myself be coaxed into sleeping with someone who just wanted to find out what I was like in bed. All you talked about was sex. You wanted me, you said, and you had to have me. Well, you can't. I'm not available.'

He seemed so stunned by what she was saying that he couldn't get a sound out. He just stared at her with silvery incredulous eyes, and Natalie decided to go before he came out of shock.

She wasn't staying here to get into a fight with him. Turning on her heel, she went back through the house to the cloakroom. Locking herself in, she dressed hurriedly with hands that shook. She was afraid that she would find Sam waiting when she came out again, but as she came out she heard the sound of his car driving away with a roar of acceleration, tyres screaming on the driveway.

Why had he left? Because he was so angry he was afraid he might actually hit her? Or was frustration sending him in search of someone else? Would he go looking for Helen West?

A knife twisted in her stomach, but she refused to be jealous. He wasn't worth it.

As she moved to the front door his mother, wearing an old blue angora dressing gown, came to the top of the stairs, peering down at her. 'Was that Sam?' she asked with a yawn. 'What did he want?'

Natalie began to laugh wildly, tears burning the back of her eyes, and his mother stared at her, startled at first, then anxious.

'My dear girl, what's wrong?' Mrs Erskine began to come down the stairs. 'Did you quarrel with Sam?'

Natalie bit down on her lower lip to stop herself laughing, to keep back her tears.

'Sorry, I have to leave, Mrs Erskine,' she managed to get out in a breathless, husky rush as the other woman reached the hall. The last thing she wanted to do was confide in his mother. 'It has been a lovely day. I enjoyed it very much, thank you. I'll just collect my painting gear, then I must go.'

Mrs Erskine opened her mouth, as if to ask questions, and Natalie desperately hurried through the kitchen and out onto the patio to pick up her easel, her canvas, her paints. Sam's mother stood watching her with a thoughtful, concerned face. Natalie could see sympathy in her eyes, and flinched from it. She didn't want Sam's mother's sympathy or pity, any more than she wanted it from Sam.

'Thank you,' she said, walking past her very fast, giving her a quick, phoney, painful smile. 'It was wonderful. The food was great and I had a marvellous time—thank you for asking me.' She was talking like a robot in a voice that was just that bit too high, too mechanical. The words meant nothing and she couldn't make them sound real. Nothing was real, not even herself.

Mrs Erskine followed her to the door, listening and no doubt drawing her own conclusions. Humiliated and embarrassed, Natalie wanted to get away before she could break down. That would be the worst. If his mother saw her cry she would feel like cutting her throat.

She piled her stuff into her car and got behind the wheel. She started the engine, then gave Mrs Erskine another of her bright, false smiles, waved at her, called, 'Thanks again,' and drove off too fast, like Sam, churning the gravel on the drive.

She didn't start to cry, though, until she had got home and was safely alone in her flat.

CHAPTER SIX

SHE woke up to a weather change; the sun was gone and sea mist dripped outside, making it impossible to see further than the other side of the street. Natalie couldn't face getting up. She stayed in bed until ten, skipped breakfast and lay staring at the ceiling, in such pain she felt as if her love for Sam was an open wound in her chest which would never heal. When she got up she had no energy, even for her usual walk down to the sea—which, in this weather, she would not have been able even to catch sight of, anyway. She showered lethargically, put on jeans and a thin white ribbed cotton sweater and then stood by the window looking out, in a dismal mood, with the whole empty day ahead of her and no idea what to do with herself.

Sundays were always lazy days, of course. As always, she had done all her housework yesterday. She wasn't hungry and couldn't be bothered to cook. Most weeks she visited her parents, but they had gone up to London to see her sister and wouldn't be back until the evening.

She switched on the TV, but there was nothing on any channel that she wanted to watch. Just cartoons for kids and a political discussion which sounded even more depressed than she was. Switching the TV off, she put a disc of Sixties pop on her music centre and curled up on the couch with a book. She couldn't concentrate on what she was reading, though; the words swam into her eyes and vanished into the maze of her brain without Natalie taking in any of it.

All she could do was think about Sam, and she did a

lot of that, facing up to the fact that she had brought all this trouble down on her own head by being mischievous the morning after the party, wearing Sam's ring and pretending to believe that they really were engaged. It was all her own fault. If she hadn't played that stupid game Sam would never have kissed her, would never have got curious about her, never have thought of trying to seduce her. The past week would never have happened. Yesterday would never have happened.

She wished to God it hadn't. Nothing in her life would ever be the same. Looking back just one week was like looking across a great abyss and knowing you couldn't go back, the past was unreachable. She was a very different person from the woman she had been a week ago. She saw life, saw the whole world, with new eyes. Falling in love had changed the landscape of her life, as an earthquake did. She no longer knew exactly where she was, and that was scary.

But you couldn't change the past by wishing; you had to deal with the way things were right now, which meant, for her, trying to work out what to do about Sam, and her job. How could she go on working for him? She was already dreading going back into work to face Sam. It would be a nightmare—how could she walk into that office, look at him, talk to him, with both of them remembering what had happened at his mother's house yesterday? Sam wouldn't forget; she would see the memory in his eyes every time he looked at her. He wouldn't give up trying to get her into bed if he thought he had the ghost of a chance.

She knew Sam so well after three years. He was tenacious, obstinate, determined—a man with a strong will and a driving ego. When he wanted something he wouldn't let go.

Natalie wasn't so confident about her own will power.

Oh, she had given up sugar in her coffee, drank skimmed milk in coffee and tea although she adored cream, and she watched what she ate, she didn't smoke and had managed to keep her temper with Sam, more or less, even when he was being infuriating, for three years—but those were such little things. She had never been tempted beyond her power to resist.

Sam could do it, though. She closed her eyes, groaning. He would have a powerful ally—her own body. Sam only had to kiss her, touch her in the right way, and he could silence her mind, make her forget her self-respect, her common sense. She would be at his mercy.

I'll have to hand in my notice! she thought, and felt a stab of anguish. How could she bear never to see him again?

Which would be worse? Seeing Sam every day, with love eating at her, knowing he didn't feel anything like that for her and dying of frustration, afraid he might see, might guess, and take advantage of her feelings to seduce her? That would be intolerable. Yet never to see him, to be locked out from his presence like Eve from the Garden of Eden, thinking of him all the time, unable to forget him?

Which would be worse?

She kept changing her mind—one minute deciding to resign and the next knowing she couldn't bear to stop seeing him. What a fool you are! she thought, despising herself for being so changeable, so weak-minded.

She went to bed that night still not able to make up her mind. But Fate took a hand.

Natalie woke up on Monday morning with an aching head, a thick head cold in the nose and a high temperature. Flu! she thought, looking at her flushed face in the bathroom mirror. She felt far too ill to go to work, and in any case it would be irresponsible to spread flu around the firm. So she rang the radio station and left a message at reception for Sam, then crawled back to bed.

She couldn't sleep. Her temperature seemed to be climbing so high she was hallucinating, and she kept sneezing and blowing her nose. An hour later, she felt so much worse that she rang her doctor, who came to see her almost immediately.

He popped a thermometer in her mouth, took her pulse, looked down her throat, at her eyes, behind her ears, took out the thermometer and looked at it with raised brows, then gave her a wry look.

''You've got a temperature of a hundred and one, and you're hatching measles.'

'Measles?' she repeated incredulously. 'I thought only kids got that?'

He shook his head. 'No, adults can get it too, and it can be far more serious in adults. Don't take it lightly. Stay in bed and drink lots of fluids—not just water, vary it. Take fruit juice, milk, weak tea. If you aren't hungry, don't eat. If you are hungry, eat sensibly—eggs, fish, fruit, no junk food, please. Sleep as much as you can. I'm going to give you a prescription for some pills to take, twice a day. If you have any new symptoms ring me. Is there anyone who will come and do your shopping, collect your pills, take care of you? Or would you like me to arrange for the district nurse to come in once a day?'

'My mother will come,' Natalie said, not wanting some strange woman coming there to fuss around her.

'Good, good—much more comfortable for you,' said the doctor, as if he knew what she had been thinking. He wrote out a prescription, handed it to her, then glanced at his watch and made a face. 'Well, must get on. Lots of other patients to see—by the way, you're the third case of measles I've seen this weekend. It must be going around. Hope I'm not going to have an epidemic on my hands! Usually get that in the winter. When the spots start fading, and you feel okay, come in and have a check-up and I'll tell you when you can go back to work.'

'How long will I be off, do you think?'

'Oh, couple of weeks—not much more than that.' Giving her a grin, the doctor said, 'Enjoy the rest—think of it as a little holiday and you'll feel better.' Shutting his black bag, he hurried out, closing the front door behind him.

Somebody heard my prayers, Natalie thought, drinking a glass of water. She had been dry-mouthed and thirsty all day. She slid out of bed to dial her parents' number, but only got the answering machine; they must be out shopping. She left a message telling them she had measles and asking if her mother could spare the time to visit her that day.

She then climbed back into bed and dozed for a while. A seagull woke her up, screeching raucously right outside her window. Yawning, Natalie realised she had to go to the bathroom and forced herself to get up again. Just moving seemed too much effort at the moment.

Before going back to bed she splashed her hot face with lukewarm water and studied herself in the mirror, wondering how soon the spots would emerge. She felt silly, catching such a childish ailment. People were going to laugh at her.

She should have asked the doctor how he knew she had measles. What had he been looking for behind the ears? Was it measles where you first got spots behind the ears? Or was that chickenpox? She had never had measles as a child but she thought she had had chickenpox. Or had it been the other way round? Could you get either of them twice? She tried to see behind her ears, using a hand mirror reflected into the bathroom mirror, but it didn't work and she couldn't feel any spots.

On her way back to bed she was startled by a peremptory ring on the doorbell. For a minute she thought of ignoring it, but whoever was out there was not giving up; the ringing continued, shrilly, making her head hurt. Who on earth…? Oh, of course. It must be her parents. They must have come straight away after hearing her recorded message.

Putting on a warm wool dressing gown and slippers, Natalie ran a brush over her tousled dark hair and went to open the door. She didn't want to scare her mother into imagining she had a mortal illness! She knew how her mother's overactive imagination could work—you sneezed and she had you in your coffin before you could sneeze again.

When she saw who stood outside she tried to shut the door again on a reflex, but Sam inserted himself into the closing space, shoving the door open again with a powerful shoulder.

'Don't be silly, Natalie, I just want to talk to you. Surely we can talk to each other like a couple of adults?'

'Go away! I'm too ill to cope with you. Just go away, will you?' Natalie wailed, but he was inside her flat and closing the door with a bang that made her flinch and clutch her head.

'A bit convenient, your illness, isn't it?' Sam demanded, staring at her. 'You were fine on Saturday, but suddenly you ring in and say you're sick and can't come to work! Is this your way of punishing me for making a pass at you? Don't tell me there's no connection, because I wouldn't believe it if you swore it on a stack of Bibles.'

'If you've come here to pick a row with me—'

'No, on the contrary. I'm here to mend fences—I

don't want to quarrel with you,' Sam interrupted hastily. 'You're the best assistant I ever had, and I need you in the office. And I'm sorry I made that pass at you. The last thing I want to do is ruin our good working relationship.'

Rage flared inside her. That was all she was to him, wasn't it? His dogsbody in the office. He regretted ever having risked their working relationship!

'Oh, just buzz off, will you?' She felt so feverish that she could not stand up any longer. The room seemed to be going round and round, as if she were in a washing machine.

She wasn't seeing Sam clearly, but she was so ill it no longer mattered. Who cared what he thought? Turning her back on him, she staggered back to her bed, sank down on it, pulled off her dressing gown and dropped it on the floor, crawled between the sheets, pulling them up over her head, and shut her eyes. The blessed darkness and silence was like a cool hand on her heated temples. She sighed blissfully.

Then she realised that there really was a cool hand on her temples. Sam's hand. His long fingers spread across her hot skin, and at once the heat inside her shot sky-high and she trembled violently.

'You've got a raging temperature!' His voice was deep; it sounded anxious. 'You really are ill, aren't you? If this is flu, you've got a bad dose of it.'

'It's measles, not flu,' she said hoarsely. Even her throat no longer seemed to work.

'Measles? That's what kids get,' he said wryly. 'Trust you to get a childish disease. I knew you hadn't properly grown up!'

He had pulled the sheet back from her face, but Natalie ignored him. Maybe he would go away if she pretended he wasn't there? Stop touching me, she thought. I like it too much.

The hand was removed. She felt Sam move away, walk across the room. Was he going? She waited for the sound of the front door closing, but instead she heard him go into the bathroom, then after a brief pause he came back, making her pulses clamour again as he sat down on the edge of her bed. She pretended to be asleep, but he ran a cool finger down her cheek to caress the curve of her parted mouth, startling her into opening her eyes in shock at that brief, sensuous contact—as light as a butterfly fluttering against her lips and yet sending shock waves down through her whole body.

'Have you taken any medicine for this?' he asked, watching her.

She didn't meet those probing eyes. She was afraid of revealing something to them.

'Aspirin, when I first woke up.'

'When was that? Eight, nine o'clock?'

She nodded, then wished she hadn't; the movement hurt her neck, made her headache worse again.

'Anything since then?'

'No,' she whispered threadily. 'Leave me alone. Go away.'

He put a hand under her shoulders and lifted her to a sitting position, holding her there with his arm behind her. 'Here, swallow this.' He held a cloudy glass to her lips.

She closed her mouth firmly and he sighed.

'Okay, don't look so suspicious. I'm not trying to drug you—this is just soluble aspirin. We have to bring this temperature down.'

She was too weak to argue; she swallowed the mixture and Sam gently laid her down again, bending so close to her that she could feel his breath on her hair. She had a crazy urge to put her arms round his neck and pull him down to her, kiss him, but of course she didn't.

'Don't get so close. You'll catch my measles,' she muttered, not even daring to look at him while he was so close to her.

His mouth moved near her ear, brushing the rim of it, making her pulses go crazy. 'The warning's too late. I've already discovered how dangerous it is to get too close to you.'

Her heart turned over. What did he mean by that? Her skin was burning; she could scarcely breathe. Had it been a joke? Or had he meant something serious? He had sounded serious, sounded dry, ironic. But what had he meant?

She was dying to see his face—that might tell her— but she wouldn't open her eyes or look at him. Why didn't he go? She wanted him out—of her flat, of her life, of her dreams. She did not want him within a mile of her bed, making her feel like this, sending wild, sensual quivers through her.

How was it physically possible to feel so ill and yet at the same time so charged with yearning? Her body was a battleground for conflicting sensations.

'What's this?' Sam asked, rustling paper. 'A prescription? Did the doctor leave it? Shouldn't you get this from the chemist at once? I'll go and collect it—give me the key to your flat, then I can let myself in when I come back with the pills.'

She had to open her eyes then. Seeing him again was anguish and delight. Haloed against the light from the window, his face was in shadow, but out of it she saw those beautiful, translucent grey eyes watching her. They were far too shrewd and alert. Whatever she did, she mustn't let him glimpse how he could make her feel.

But it was very hard to manage when she felt so weak. She wished he would go. And soon.

Her voice thick and husky, she quickly said, 'Thank you, but there's no need for you to bother. My mother's coming to take care of me. She should be here any minute. You'd better go before she gets here.'

'I'd like to meet her. You've never told me much about your family, apart from mentioning a married sister.'

'You always said we should keep our personal lives out of the office!'

He looked down at her, his lashes against his cheek, his eyes glinting behind them seductively. 'This isn't the office,' he pointed out, mouth curling in a teasing smile that made her heart turn over again. Why did he have so much charm? It wasn't fair. 'Are you like your mother?'

She shrugged. 'A little, I suppose, to look at—but my sister is more like her in character.'

'Not a crosspatch when she's ill, like you, then?' he mocked.

Natalie gave him a cold look and let her lids droop as if she was going to sleep. But she watched him through her lashes, her mouth dry. He was wearing one of his office suits, a lightweight summer one, a whiteish cotton striped with pale grey; it was so thin you could see how lean he was, especially as his white shirt was slightly opaque in the sunlight and showed her his body underneath, an outline of his ribcage, the muscular form of his chest.

The sunlight also glinted on his black lashes, giving them gold tips. It gave his lightly tanned skin a golden glow, made his eyes a brilliant silver.

'Have you had lunch?' he asked her, and she opened her eyes reluctantly, shook her head.

'I'm not hungry.'

'I am, and you ought to have something. When you're ill, going without food doesn't help, you know. You should have something light and digestible.'

She gave him an incredulous look. 'Stop talking like my mother!'

'Am I? Obviously she and I are going to get on well! I can't wait to meet her.'

She didn't want them to meet at all. Her mother would immediately pick up on her feelings, and probe away until she knew exactly what was going on.

'Oh, don't feel you have to wait until my mother gets here,' she quickly said. 'Go and have lunch, Sam.'

'Have you got any food here?'

'I'll be okay; I did some shopping on Saturday. If I do get hungry I'll have a wide choice.'

He got up, the springs of her bed giving. She watched him walk away, but he only went as far as her little kitchenette, where he began coolly opening cupboards.

'What do you think you're doing?' Natalie asked, exasperated into sitting up, eyes wide open now.

He turned, taking off his jacket and hanging it over a chair. 'How about an omelette? I often cook one for myself. You've got eggs, cheese, some salad—you can have a choice of cheese or tomato omelette.'

'I'm not hungry!' Flushed and irritated, she slid out of bed. 'Do I have to throw you out myself? Please, go away, Sam. I can take care of myself.'

It might have been more impressive if she hadn't tripped over her own slippers and stumbled. Sam caught her before she measured her length on the floor. She fell against him, her face buried in his shirt, and felt his arms close around her. His heart was beating strongly under her mouth; she shut her eyes and leaned on him, mouth parted as if she were kissing him, breathing in the scent of his body.

It couldn't have taken more than a few seconds, but it felt as if eternity flashed past, then Sam lifted her off her feet and put her back into her bed, pulling her bed-clothes up and tucking them in.

She felt like a little girl being put to bed by her daddy; it was both comforting and disturbing. She couldn't help enjoying the sensation of being cosseted and taken care of—yet at the same time she was afraid of enjoying it too much. She knew there was no future in this rela-tionship, except for it to continue as it had done ever since she'd started working for him. Sam wanted a good assistant. Nothing else was on offer except a brief af-fair—a little light amusement for him, and heartbreak for her.

Sam straightened and walked away without a word. Natalie stared after him. Was he leaving? No, he had gone back into the bathroom. He came out almost at once. She hurriedly shut her eyes again. Sam sat down on her bed and began gently wiping her face with a dampened towel, stroking it over her forehead, her cheeks, her neck.

She couldn't help the groan of pleasure that escaped her. The coolness on her hot skin was wonderful, espe-cially whenever Sam's fingers touched her, as they kept doing, brushing her closed eyelids, her cheekbones, her ears, her lips, where they lingered for a second or two.

'Now...that omelette? Cheese or tomato?' he asked, his voice husky.

'Tomato,' she weakly said, giving up the argument because he had sapped her every last ounce of energy. She couldn't fight him any more, not now, not with him so close, watching her with that intent grey gaze. What was going on behind those eyes? What was he thinking?

They had worked together for three years, often alone for hours in one room, yet she had never felt this strange, quiveringly intense intimacy with him before.

The man she knew at work was somehow different. Sam could be brusque, sharp, thoughtful, hard, shrewd— a clever man with a mind like quicksilver and a dry sense of humour.

She had never suspected that he could be tender, kind and thoughtful, too, that she would be so comfortable with him when she was ill. She knew how crotchety she could be when she had so much as a bad cold. Her mother had often complained that she reverted to six years old at the drop of a hat whenever she was off colour. Yet Sam seemed to take that in his stride, amused rather than annoyed by her cross mood.

'Got any herbs?' he asked, and she nodded.

'On the windowsill. I grow a few—chives, basil, mint.'

He found the small terracotta pot, divided like a wheel to keep the various herbs apart, and picked a little basil and snipped off chives.

'These will be perfect!'

As one hypnotised, she watched him beat the eggs, chop some tomatoes, slice another couple of tomatoes and pop them under the grill, grate a little of the cheese, heat butter in a pan, pour in the eggs and lightly move them around with a fork before adding the tomatoes and the herbs. She was impressed by his speed and dexterity. He really knew what he was doing and he could cook; she would never have expected that. He wasn't the type of man she had ever thought would turn out to cook well.

The scent of the food made her nostrils quiver. The smell was actually making her hungry! Sam flipped the omelette over, slid it out onto a plate he had warmed under the grill, then cut it in half. He brought a tray over to the bed two minutes later; each of them had half an omelette, with grilled sliced tomatoes sprinkled with a little grated cheese and what was left of the fresh herbs.

Natalie sat up with some pillows behind her back and slowly began to eat; Sam ate sitting on the end of her bed with his plate on his knee.

'This is really terrific!' Natalie said halfway through her omelette, taking a sip of the glass of orange juice he had brought her.

'I know,' he said complacently. 'I was taught by a French girl I once dated. She was a chef and hated cooking except at work, so she taught me to cook for her.'

Natalie's brows shot up. 'You're kidding!'

'No, it's true.'

'You did the cooking for a girlfriend?'

'Well, I learnt to cook, and I taught her a thing or two in return.'

Their eyes met, his bright with self-mockery and teasing, and she laughed croakily—although she hated the thought of what he would have taught the French girl. She was only just discovering how jealousy could hurt.

'I suppose she was gorgeous?' Just asking the question was like sticking a knife into herself. She didn't want to know the answer, but she didn't want him to realise she was so jealous.

'You sound like a frog!' he told her, amused, taking her empty plate. 'You're getting a bad throat.' As he walked away with the plate he said casually over his shoulder, 'And, yes, Yvette was gorgeous—small skinny and dark. Very French; she wore cheap, simple clothes as if they were designer gear—skimpy tunics, black, very short. They showed a lot of her. Her legs weren't as great as yours, but she was chic and, after a few lessons from me, very sexy.'

Natalie restrained an urge to put out her tongue; it

would have been childish and would have revealed her jealousy. 'How long ago did you know her?'

Where had this Yvette come in the list of his girl-friends? was really what she wanted to know. And also, Exactly how many girlfriends had he had? But she wouldn't descend to asking. She wouldn't give him the satisfaction.

'Oh, I was still at college—that was where I met her; she was over here learning English. She was nineteen, I was twenty. I thought I was a man of the world, to be dating a sophisticated French girl, but actually we were both innocents, of course.' Sam grinned at her. 'That was a long time ago.'

'A long, long time, if you were only twenty!' she bit back, and saw his brows lift at her cross tone.

'You are in a tetchy mood today,' he said, sliding their plates into hot water. 'But I'm glad to see that you were hungrier than you thought. You ate every scrap. Pity there was no wine, but the orange juice was probably better for you.'

'Better for you, too. You don't want to drink too much again, do you?'

He eyed her drily. 'Your tongue's very sharp today. There's a very waspish side to your character I never noticed before.'

'You never noticed me at all!' she muttered.

'I did, you know.'

At once she was dying to know what he had noticed, and he knew that, grinning at her. But he didn't en-lighten her. He left her in suspense, and she furiously knew he did that deliberately.

'I'll go and get that prescription for you now,' he said. 'It doesn't look as if your mother is coming—shall I ring her for you?'

'I'll do it,' she said, preparing to slide out of bed, but Sam pushed her back onto her pillows.

'You stay where you are!'

She lay back, glaring at him. 'Stop ordering me around, will you?'

'When you stop doing stupid things!' His voice was calm, infuriatingly reasonable. 'You're ill, Natalie. Try to be sensible. You must stay in bed and rest.' He picked up her handbag from the chair by her bed. 'Now, give me your front door key. Is there anything else I can get you from the shops? You're going to run low on orange juice soon. I'll get you some—what else? Fruit? Milk, eggs, cheese?'

'Thank you,' she said meekly, hunting in her bag for her front door key and handing it to him.

'I won't be long. Lie back and rest while I'm gone. Don't try and ring your mother, do you hear?'

When he had gone Natalie lay back on her pillows, thinking. This is so surreal. It can't be happening. Was she hallucinating? Now that Sam had left she half believed she had imagined his visit—perhaps he had never been there, had never cooked her a meal and such a terrific meal, an omelette better than any Natalie had ever cooked for herself. Had he really sat on her bed and eaten his half of the food, cleared their plates away, scolding her and cosseting her as if he were her father? No, it couldn't have happened. She had dreamt it all, hadn't she?

Any minute now her mother would arrive and break the spell. She looked at her bedside clock. Come to think of that, where on earth was her mother? It was hours since she'd rung home. Her heart jumped into her throat. Something must be wrong—why else hadn't they got her message and rung back, if they weren't coming?

Her imagination began working feverishly. What if

the car had crashed on their way back from London? They could be lying in a hospital somewhere, unconscious.

But someone would have rung her. The police would have traced the ownership of the car, and neighbours would have told them where she lived. They all knew her.

The telephone began to ring and she leapt up in bed, heart beating violently. Stumbling out of bed, she ran across the room to snatch up the phone.

'Nat?' It was her mother's voice, and at once she slumped in relief, breathing raggedly.

'Mum...where are you?'

'At home. We had been to lunch with the MacDonalds and I only just found your message on the machine. How are you, darling? You sound very rough. Measles! That can make you very ill, at your age. Are the spots out yet?'

'No, not yet. I'm a bit feverish and I have a terrible head cold, but I'm not as ill as I was this morning.'

'That's good—I hope you're staying in bed, though, and drinking lots of fluid. How's your appetite?'

'I just ate a tomato omelette and drank a lot of orange juice, so you needn't worry about my appetite! And there's no need for you to come over now, Mum. I'm very sleepy anyway. There's nothing you could do.'

'Are you sure? Dad has gone to have his nap, but I can drive over to you if you need me, Nat.'

'No—I suppose I was in a bit of a panic when I rang you. Being told you've got measles when you feel too grown-up to have it has that effect, but I'm used to the idea now, and I'm feeling much better.'

'Well, if you're sure... I'll come over tomorrow morning, darling, and if you need me before that give me a ring.'

'Thanks, I will,' Natalie said gratefully. When she had rung off she visited the bathroom. As she climbed back into bed a couple of minutes later the front doorbell rang. It must be Sam—had he forgotten that he had her key? She put on her dressing gown and hurried to the door, but when she opened it she was confronted by an enormous bouquet of long-stemmed, dark red roses.

Her heart crashed. Sam had bought her red roses!

But it wasn't Sam. It was Johnny who peered round them, grinning at her. 'Hi, sweetheart! They told me you were ill so I came round to bring you these.' His other hand came up, proffering a basket of fruit. 'And this.'

Fighting disappointment, Natalie smiled waveringly at him, noting that he wasn't wearing his usual black leather. Today he was wearing black jeans and a white sweater, and looked even sexier than usual.

'What lovely roses; you are kind, Johnny.' She accepted the bouquet and took the basket of fruit in the other hand. 'What a marvellous selection of fruit—a whole pineapple, and strawberries, and cherries! Exactly what I need at the moment. You're very thoughtful, thanks.' Stepping back, she said, 'Do you want to come in?'

'You aren't contagious, are you?' he asked, keeping well back from her. 'What's wrong, exactly? Susie told me, the girl at Reception, but she didn't seem sure what was wrong. She thought you had said flu, but she'd forgotten.'

'Measles,' Natalie said, and he looked at her, amazed, then laughed.

'You're kidding! I didn't know adults could get that.'

'Well, they can, and I have. Did you have it when you were a child, Johnny? Because if you didn't, you had better keep well away from me. It's very contagious.'

'Oh, I had it when I was six, and I'm pretty sure you can't catch it twice. I had everything,' he boasted, walking past her into the flat. 'Mumps, chickenpox, measles—I caught everything that was going at school. I was always off sick; I was one of those kids. I spent more time away than I did at school. My mother had me into bed and was calling the doctor if I so much as sneezed.' He looked around at the tumbled bed, the tiny kitchenette, the bathroom door. 'So, this is your flat?'

'It isn't very big, but I can't afford anything bigger on my salary. I'm lucky to have got this place so cheaply. It has a great view.'

Natalie looked for her one and only big vase, a very cheap earthenware one, white with a pattern of dark green leaves trailing around it. It had been a housewarming present from her sister; Natalie would never have thought of buying herself a vase, she had only bought necessary items, like pots and pans. Yet she had found herself using Bethany's vase often; flowers brightened the room, made the flat feel more like a home. She didn't often buy flowers, but whenever she visited her parents they gave her flowers, picked from their garden, or Natalie found wild flowers when she was out walking in the countryside near their home. She loved to bring back bluebells in spring, and, as summer arrived, pink campion, honey-scented meadowsweet, tall, pink, swaying willowherb.

Filling the vase with water, she stripped leaves from the stems of the roses before putting them into the vase, which she carried over to the windowsill.

'I'll be able to see them properly here and they will cheer me up every time I look at them. Thank you,' she told Johnny. 'Can I get you a cup of coffee?'

He looked at his watch, shaking his head. 'No, I can't stop. I just wanted to see how you were, then I'm driving up to London to see someone.' He turned wide, appealing, boyish eyes on her. 'Have you forgiven me yet? For Friday night?'

She couldn't help laughing. If she had been in love with Johnny he might have broken her heart last Friday night, but all he had done was annoy her a little, so she told him, 'Yes, I forgive you, Johnny—although I wish that photo hadn't got into the paper. It made me look half-witted.'

'You always look gorgeous, even when you've got measles,' Johnny said, then he took her hand and bowed over it as if he were kissing it. He didn't, however, Natalie noted, he kissed the air above it—which was typical of Johnny. He was a man who lived on the surface of things; creating images was his style, not feeling deeply. That was the way he was made; you couldn't blame him for being what nature had made him.

But she didn't have time to think much more because before Johnny had straightened up, while he was still holding her hand and apparently kissing it, a key turned in the lock of her front door, the door opened and Sam stood there, staring at them with hard, narrowed eyes.

CHAPTER SEVEN

HEARING the door open, Johnny looked round and stared, wide-eyed. 'Sam?' he gasped and his jaw dropped ludicrously, as if someone had hit him in the stomach. Then he looked back at Natalie, staring as if she had suddenly grown two heads.

'What are you doing here?' asked Sam in an iceberg voice.

Johnny's fallen angel face flushed in confusion. She could see at that second how he must have looked as a teenager; Johnny had not always been the sophisticated, streetwise guy his fans worshipped, she thought, touched by the image of him twenty years younger. Poor Johnny, how he was hating growing middle-aged.

'I heard Natalie was sick, so I came by to see how she was doing,' he told Sam, whose face did not unfreeze.

'She needs peace and quiet, not visitors.'

'Oh, sure—of course,' Johnny hurriedly said. 'I was just going. Hope you get better soon, Natalie, we'll all miss you at work.' His eyes didn't quite meet hers, though, and there was an embarrassed flush on his face which baffled her for a second, until it dawned on her what Johnny was thinking.

Sam had let himself in with a key and was openly displeased to find Johnny there. Remembering Sam had proposed to her at his party, Johnny was putting two and two together and making a hundred; he now believed that she and Sam were lovers, had secretly been lovers for a long time.

Natalie felt a bubble of hysterical laughter form in her throat, but she was furious, too. She didn't want gossip like that spreading around the radio station—but would Johnny believe her if she explained that Sam just had the key briefly, because he had gone to get her prescription? Oh, he would pretend to believe it, but he would be bound to think she was lying, covering up. She should never have given her key to Sam. Now look what he had let them both in for!

Johnny turned to leave, and found himself on the receiving end of one of Sam's blackest scowls. As Sam was still standing just inside the flat Johnny had to pass him to escape, and he hesitated.

He was reluctant to run the gauntlet of Sam's displeasure, and how could blame him when Sam looked like that?

'The show went well this morning,' offered Johnny, trying one of his charming little-boy smiles. 'Lots of calls—always a good sign.' If he thought he would placate Sam with that he was in for a disappointment. Sam was not softened by the little-boy look Johnny switched on and off so easily. That only worked with women. Men were impervious to Johnny's charm.

Natalie watched them both wryly, understanding that Johnny didn't quite know how to get himself out of the flat. He needed a cue.

'I'll be able to listen to your programme at home tomorrow,' she said softly, and Johnny's face lit up gratefully.

'So you will! You do that, sweetheart—and I'll dedicate a song to you. What would you like me to play?'

'Anything will do,' she said, carefully not glancing in Sam's direction but feeling the vibrations of his rage from where she stood. Sam didn't want Johnny dedicating songs to her on air.

Johnny could feel it too, and decided to make a run for it. 'Okay, leave it to me. I'll pick something for you. Well, see you—take care of yourself,' he said, rushing at the door, adding nervously, 'Bye, Sam.'

'Goodbye,' Sam said, slamming the door shut the second Johnny was through it.

'Now look what you've done!' Natalie croaked at him.

'What I've done?' Sam came towards her, his lip curling in a sneer. 'What have you been up to while I was out? What was going on when I arrived? I saw him kissing your hand—had he just started a pass or did I miss the rest?'

Having him come so close made her intensely edgy, but Natalie wasn't backing off; she was too angry and she wouldn't give him the satisfaction of knowing he could alarm her. She glared right back at him, her chin up and defiance glittering in her eyes. 'You missed him giving me flowers and a basket of fruit—that's all you missed! And it was very kind and thoughtful of him to bring them! You didn't bring me flowers, did you? Or a very expensive basket of fruit, either!'

'I'm not trying to get into your bed!'

Scarlet, she hissed back. 'Neither was Johnny! He was just being kind.'

Sam laughed angrily. 'Come off it! I know him— that's how he operates. Mr Nice Guy always has a long-term agenda, and it always involves getting into some girl's bed.'

'Sure you aren't talking about yourself?'

He stared at her as if doubting his ears. 'Me? I hope that was a joke, Natalie. I don't spend my time trying to seduce every woman I meet!'

'Oh, it was just a rumour, then?' she snapped, and his eyes flashed.

'You shouldn't listen to gossip! It's usually exaggerated, if not an outright lie.'

'Talking about gossip,' she said coldly, 'Johnny didn't miss the fact that you used a key to get into my flat, you know! Now he thinks you always have a key, and he'll be on the phone for the rest of the day, spreading that gossip. By the time you go back to the office everyone in the building will know. Any hope we had of people forgetting about you proposing at Johnny's party is dead in the water! Everyone is going to think we're an item and have been for ages, secretly.'

Sam's eyes widened; the lines on his forehead bit deeper. 'That didn't occur to me. You're right. Damn it! Why didn't you tell Linklater why I had your key?'

'I didn't think he would believe me.'

Sam's mouth twisted. 'No, I don't suppose he would. But it's your fault, not mine!'

'My fault!' she gasped, then said with biting sarcasm, 'Of course I knew it would be, but just for curiosity's sake, tell me—how do you make that out?'

'You should never have let him in! Then he wouldn't have been here to see me use your front door key, would he?' The man never admitted being in the wrong—she should have remembered that! His mother was a lovely woman, and Natalie liked her a lot, but she had spoilt him, let him grow up thinking he was the centre of the universe and lord of all he surveyed.

Coldly, Natalie said, 'I should never have given you my key, you mean! Which reminds me—I saw you put it in your pocket—can I have it back, please? I don't want you going off with it.' He was capable of it, capable of letting himself in and out of her flat as if he owned the place, and she wasn't standing for that.

She put her hand out with an insistent stare, and, still frowning, he got the key out of his pocket and slapped it into her palm. Natalie picked up her bag and put the key back into it, asking him, 'Did you get my medicine?'

He was carrying a plastic bag in one hand; he put it on the top of her kitchen cabinet and began getting the contents out: first a chemist's bag, which must be her pills, then a bottle of orange juice. Over his shoulder he growled, 'Get into bed! You should never have got out. I told you to stay in bed until I got back, didn't I?'

She was tempted to refuse, but she was feeling weak-kneed again, and bed was a tempting prospect. All the same, she didn't move at once, in case he thought he had some right to order her around. Not that Sam needed much encouragement to be dictatorial—at work he tended to snap orders at everyone, male or female. Some of the engineers called him The Great Dictator; some of them used far ruder descriptions. It was all that adrenalin in his veins, all that testosterone—he needed it in order to run the company as well as he did, to give him the edge over other men, and it didn't switch off when he wasn't at work.

'I had to get out of bed to open the front door, didn't I?'

'No, you didn't! You should have ignored the doorbell. Then Linklater would never have been here to see me come in with your key!'

He took out a bottle of still mineral water from his bag, poured some of it into a glass and got out a strip of metal-enfolded capsules from the chemist's bag. He pushed one out and offered her it, holding out the glass of water. 'Take this, then get into bed.'

'Oh, stop yelling orders at me!' she muttered, but took the capsule and swallowed it with some water, then took off her dressing gown and got into bed, watched closely by Sam.

She wished he wouldn't stare like that; her nightdress

wasn't transparent, but the fact that that was all she was wearing made her very self-conscious—or rather, very conscious of being alone with Sam, and in bed, wearing so little.

He put the bottle of water on her bedside table with the glass. 'I ought to be getting back to work—anything else I can do for you first? Shall I ring your mother to find out when she can get here?'

'She rang while you were out.'

'And she's coming?'

'Yes,' she evaded—it wasn't exactly a lie as her mother *would* be coming tomorrow. If she told Sam her mother wasn't coming today he might insist on returning after work, to make sure she was okay, and she did not want that. She was on edge while he was here. She couldn't relax, and she was feeling drained and exhausted now; she needed to sleep—which she couldn't do with Sam there.

'Will she stay here?' Sam glanced around the little apartment. 'There's nowhere for her to sleep. I suppose she'll go back home this evening? She lives miles away, doesn't she?'

'Only ten miles—it doesn't take long.'

'Driving back and forth will be tiring for her.'

'I think I'll go back with her and stay until I'm better.' She shrugged. 'Thanks for coming and looking after me, for cooking my lunch—it was delicious. I had no idea you could cook like that.'

'That's okay. You look tired, get some sleep when I've gone.'

She nodded. 'Okay—bye, Sam.'

He still stood by the bed, looking down at her, and she feverishly wished he would go.

'If you do go to your parents, let me know,' he said, still not moving, and Natalie couldn't meet his eyes because she was so aware of him. She kept thinking he was going to bend and kiss her, and she wanted that so badly it hurt.

But he didn't, for which she tried to be relieved. He turned abruptly on his heel and walked to the front door while she lay in bed and watched him, feeling blank and cold and on the point of tears.

'I'll be seeing you,' Sam said, glancing back once, his face unreadable, and then the front door shut on him and she was alone again.

That was when she cried, silently, her eyes shut and the tears trickling down her face like rain down a window.

She fell asleep crying, and cried in her sleep, in a dream of Sam. He was walking away from her through the familiar corridors of the radio station and she was running after him, sobbing, but Sam kept disappearing into rooms which, when she got there, were always empty. People turned and stared at her curiously. She ran on, calling Sam's name, but she never caught up with him, and when she woke up she was still crying.

It was quite dark and she must have been asleep for a long time because after lying awake for a while she noticed the room lightening again and realised it must be approaching dawn. Turning her head on the pillow, she looked at her alarm clock; it was almost five.

Her temperature had broken, but her bed was damp with perspiration and so was her nightdress. She got up and had a shower, put on a clean nightdress, changed the sheets on her bed, had some orange juice and a cup of hot chocolate. She felt light and cool and calm as she watched dawn breaking over the sea—first a roseate glow which became a golden light spreading along the horizon. Below was the sea, very blue, and white gulls lazily coasting on a warm spiral of air.

The morning air had a touch of chill about it, though, so she got back into bed and soon fell asleep again. This time she slept without dreaming, or, if she dreamt, did not remember her dreams when she woke up. Yawning, she stretched her arms, looked at the clock and was startled to find it was half past nine. She hadn't slept like this for a long, long time.

She felt so well that she actually ate some breakfast after washing and putting on a pair of jeans and a thin blue sweater, and her temperature was still more or less normal when her mother arrived. Natalie hadn't looked in the mirror that morning, so it was Mrs Craig, about to kiss her cheek, who spotted the first telltale spots and pointed them out to Natalie, who rushed to the bathroom to stare at herself in a mirror.

There was a sprinkling of red dots across her face and on her neck. As she stared at them she was sure they spread even as she watched, multiplying like rabbits across her face.

She groaned. 'Oh, why did this have to happen to me? How on earth did I catch it? How long do the spots last, Mum? I'll have to hide until they've gone! And I was feeling so much better this morning. I was breathing more or less normally and my temperature was down!'

'That's normal,' her mother said cheerfully. 'Once the spots come out you do feel better. It's while you're hatching them that you feel ill and you're so contagious!'

Darkly Natalie hoped Sam had caught her measles when he'd kissed her yesterday.

'You'll be off work for a few weeks, I imagine,' her mother added. 'Dad suggested I brought you back with me. You don't want to be here alone, when you're ill. I'll pack a case for you, then we'll drive home. I've got your room aired and ready for you. You'll be much more comfortable there and I can take care of you.'

'Thanks, Mum,' Natalie said gratefully.

An hour later she was tucked up in bed in the spare room of her parents' bungalow while her mother was in the kitchen preparing a meal she regarded as suitable for an invalid. Her father had opened the door for them, kissed Natalie and asked her anxiously how she was. After she had told him she was much better today, he'd carried her case into the little room at the end of the bungalow. It was very quiet there, looking out into the garden; the window stood open to let in fresh air, sunlight and the sounds of birds singing in the trees. When her father had gone off to make some coffee, Natalie got undressed and into the bed.

Her father brought her a cup of coffee and a couple of home-made shortbread biscuits and sat and talked to her for a few minutes, his talk wandering from the weather to the latest tennis news, from the new strain of gooseberry bush he was growing to a complaint about the sudden eruption of greenfly which had hit his roses and against which he was waging a bitter war.

From the kitchen her mother called, 'That girl should be resting, not listening to you!'

Guiltily, her father got up. 'I forgot you were ill!'

'I was enjoying the chance of a chat,' protested Natalie.

'No, no, your mother's right, she always is. You should be resting, not listening to me chattering on and on.'

He kissed the top of her head and left, closing the door behind him. Natalie lay back with a sigh of pleasure, looking around the room. She often stayed here, although this bungalow had not been the home in which she grew up, and the room was very familiar to her.

Square, decorated in calming shades of green, with chintz curtains and light pine furniture, it was springlike and lifted her spirits.

Her mother had lit a log fire in the hearth to dry up any dampness in the room, since it was rarely in use. An old ash tree growing on the edge of the rambling garden had been blown down by a strong spring gale some months ago and her parents were still burning the logs, which saved them a fortune in fuel. They had central heating which was fed by a solid fuel Aga; they burned not only logs and coal in it but any household refuse which could not be recycled. It was a very cheap way of heating the house.

Johnny's red roses, standing on top of the little chest of drawers across the room from her bed, luxuriously scented the air. She had forgotten them, but as they'd left the flat her mother had exclaimed, 'You can't leave those lovely roses to die! We must take them with us!' and rushed back to take them out of their vase, shake their wet stems in the sink and wrap them in newspaper.

She had popped the basket of fruit into her car, too, and it stood now on Natalie's bedside table, within easy reach, tempting her to take a handful of the glossy red cherries. She ate them slowly and threw the stones out into the garden. It would be nice if one of them rooted; she liked the idea of a cherry tree growing outside the window.

Her mother brought her lunch on a tray, refusing to let her get up. She had cooked a delicate fillet of sole, gently poached in milk, a few tiny new potatoes, spinach and thin strips of carrot, followed by ice-cream, home-made by Mrs Craig with raspberries from her own garden, with fresh raspberries trickled over the top.

It was the perfect meal for Natalie's state of health;

she ate almost all of it, telling her mother, 'It was wonderful, Mum, absolutely delicious.'

Mrs Craig smiled, pleased. Then, drawing the curtains but leaving the window a little open, she told Natalie firmly she should have another nap, and went away with the tray. Lying in the shady, quiet room, Natalie found it easy to drift off into a light doze.

The weather remained fine all that week, and Natalie spent it peacefully in bed, in her little room, with just one sheet over her, and pillows banked up for her head, resting and eating the light meals her mother made her, reading books her father got her from the rural mobile library which stopped just down the road once a week. It didn't have a huge selection of books, but if there was something you badly wanted they would get it for you next time they came, if possible, and they did carry a wide range, from novels to biographies to books on how to do everything under the sun—including taxidermy, her father told her sadly, because her mother would never let him try that, and bee-keeping, something he *had* been allowed to pursue.

He had some hives right at the bottom of the garden, behind a hedge of hydrangeas and within easy flying distance of a field of clover which bees could enjoy. Swathed in black netting and bee-keeping gear, her father went off every day to talk to his bees and sometimes came back with honeycomb, which they then had for tea.

'It gives him a hobby and we both love honey,' Mrs Craig said.

Natalie listened to Johnny's programme every day, and smilingly heard him dedicate songs to her. 'I'm playing this for a spotty friend,' he said one day, before putting on a jokey record, and another day, 'For a beautiful girl called Natalie, who is sick. Get well soon. I miss you,' he said, then played a slow, very romantic song.

Her parents were impressed, and curious. 'I didn't realise you knew Johnny Linklater so well,' her mother said, trying not to sound too excited. 'Have you been seeing him out of work?'

'No,' Natalie said, grinning at her.

Her mother looked disappointed. 'Then why is he dedicating songs to you all the time?'

'Two songs in a week, Mum! Don't make a federal case out of it!'

Confused, her mother said, 'What?'

'Johnny's just a nice guy, and very kind-hearted,' Natalie said, relieved that she had never told her mother who'd given her the red roses—although her mother had asked several times, dying to know. If her mother knew it had been Johnny she would be planning the wedding by now, and buying herself a wedding outfit.

There had been no sign of Sam. He might at least have rung to see how she was! What had made her think he would? Out of sight, out of mind, thought Natalie bitterly. He probably had a new girlfriend and was far too busy with her to think about anything else.

Who was doing her job? If Sam had picked her she would be pretty—he must have borrowed somebody else's secretary because whoever it was would need to know a considerable amount about the way the radio station worked. He couldn't just import a temporary secretary from an agency and expect her to pick up the threads of Natalie's work.

Whoever was doing her job this week could also be Sam's latest date, of course—she tormented herself with that idea for a while, trying to work out which of the pretty girls who worked in the building had caught his eye. She could ring one of her friends at work and chat casually in the hope of being told what Sam was up to—gossip was rife around the offices, and everyone would know what was going on—but her self-respect wouldn't let her be so obvious.

By the weekend her cold vanished, her spots began to fade, she no longer had headaches and she felt so much better that she became restless with frustrated energy, sick of staying in bed and eager to get back to normal life.

The weather was almost tropical: cloudless blue skies, sunshine all day, with a distant rumble of summer thunder at times behind the deep green woods which bounded the horizon on one side of the little bungalow. Natalie went out into the garden after breakfast early on Saturday morning and spent a couple of hours lying on a deep-cushioned lounger, her head shaded by a yellow fringed sunshade.

Her father was gardening nearby and sometimes chatted to her, and her mother came out once with a tall glass of iced fruit juice and stayed for a few minutes to talk about something she had just heard on the radio. Birds flew across the garden; a cuckoo called somewhere from the secret woods. The atmosphere was drowsy, tranquil. Natalie had a book on her lap which she tried to read, but her eyelids grew heavy and in the end she succumbed to sleep, the book dropping to the grass beside her lounger.

She dreamt of Sam bending over her, kissing her, a dream so intense that when a sharp sound woke her up she was trembling violently as she opened her eyes in time to see Mrs Erskine tiptoeing away across the grass.

'Oh...hello...' Natalie said in confusion, very pink, as if Sam's mother might be able to see into her head and know what she had been dreaming about.

Mrs Erskine turned back with an apologetic smile.

'Oh, did I wake you up? I'm so sorry, Natalie. I was trying not to make a sound but I trod on a twig. What a pity—you were sleeping so peacefully, too.'

Natalie didn't know where to look. Her sleep had not been peaceful; it had been hot with dreams.

'I rang Sam and he said you were staying with your parents to convalesce, which is so sensible of you— much nicer than staying alone in a little flat,' Mrs Erskine said, sitting down on a garden chair which Mrs Craig had been sitting in earlier. She turned her face up to the sky, sighing. 'Isn't it lovely here? What a beautiful garden.'

Natalie smiled at her, lying back in the shade of the fringed umbrella again. 'My father is retired now; he spends most days out here, working.'

'It shows. Gardens are hard work; if you neglect them they run wild.'

'You have a lovely garden, too. I had a wonderful time last Saturday, Mrs Erskine. It was fun, painting with you.'

'I enjoyed it, too. How are you feeling, Natalie? I was so sorry to hear you weren't well. You must have been hatching measles last Saturday, but you didn't seem ill.'

'I thought I had a bad cold—flu, I thought—until the doctor told me it was measles. I haven't had it badly, thank heavens. I should be back at work next week.'

'I shouldn't be in any hurry. If you go back too soon you can get complications. Make sure you're really well before you start work again.'

'Sam might not agree with you,' Natalie said, trying to sound casual but hoping Mrs Erskine was going to tell her who was working for Sam in the office, and whether or not Sam had a new girlfriend.

His mother clicked her tongue. 'Oh, Sam! Who cares what he thinks?' She opened a woven straw shopping basket and brought out a couple of paperback books. 'You said you liked detective stories, so I brought you two new ones—I hope you haven't read them.'

Natalie took them and glanced at their covers. 'No, I haven't. Thank you—how kind.' She put them on the grass beside her lounger and had another try at getting information. 'How is Sam?'

'He's fine, I suppose. I don't know—I haven't seen him this week. That's why I rang him. He sounded busy and distracted.'

Distracted by whom? thought Natalie with a sinking heart.

'Did you tell him you were coming to see me?'

'I mentioned it, and he wasn't very encouraging—said I should let you recuperate, you wouldn't want visitors when you were ill—but I thought I would just call round with the books and see how you were. And your mother opened the door and said you'd love to have a visitor, you were getting very bored.'

'She's right, I am.' Natalie grimaced. 'Bored and rest-less.'

'That's a good sign—it means you're nearly better!'

At that second Mrs Craig came out with a tray of coffee which she placed on the white ironwork garden table close to Natalie's lounger. 'Oh, she is better,' she told Sam's mother. 'She's started to drive me crazy; I hate this fidgety phase of an illness. She was always the same as a child. One minute she'd be at death's door and I'd be terrified she was seriously ill, and the next she would be whining and complaining and trying to get out to play.'

'Sam was the same, only worse; he was so crotchety when he was recovering from anything. He hated being cooped up indoors. He had far too much imagination, that was one problem—the things he thought of doing!

Thank heavens I only had one son. My two girls were much easier to deal with than Sam ever was!'

'Have you got any grandchildren yet? My other daughter, Bethany, has a little boy, two now, and he can be quite a problem in the right mood.'

'I can't wait for grandchildren,' Mrs Erskine sighed, and both women looked at Natalie, who flushed and looked away.

They needn't look at her like that! Mrs Erskine's yearning for grandchildren was nothing to do with her. She picked up her coffee and began to drink it, and the two women went on talking.

Natalie stopped listening. Her heart was tender at the image of Sam as a naughty boy. Her mind drifted away to other images of Sam: Sam kissing her, Sam bellowing angrily, Sam laughing, teasing her, Sam touching her with desire. Her heartbeat was so fast she felt sick, then she heard her name and looked dazedly at Sam's mother, who was watching her with a frown.

'Natalie? Is anything wrong? Don't you feel well?'

'I'm fine,' Natalie said hurriedly, very flushed. She must be more careful—she didn't want to give herself away to his mother. Or to her own.

'Mrs Erskine was saying goodbye to you,' her mother reproached her. 'She has to go.'

Getting up, Sam's mother bent to kiss Natalie's cheek. 'I'm glad to see you're so much better. Now, be a sensible girl, don't go back to work too soon. Sam has a very capable girl doing your job.'

'Who?' Natalie asked, trying to sound casual.

'Ellen somebody, I think—or was it Helen? Anyway, he doesn't need you—he told me so—you don't need to worry. Wait until you're fully recovered before you even think about going back.'

Natalie smiled brightly at being told Sam didn't need

her. 'Oh, good,' she said, through teeth that hurt from
the tension of being gripped in a pretended smile. Sam
did not need her. It was official. He had told his mother
and his mother had told her—not that she had needed to
be told. She had known all along that Sam did not need
her. She wished bitterly that she didn't need Sam. But
she did.

Ellen? she thought, then. There was nobody working
at the radio station called Ellen. Nobody called Helen
either. It couldn't be Helen West who had stepped into
her job, could it?

Oh, don't be ridiculous! she told herself. Helen West
wouldn't work as a secretary for Sam—it would be be-
neath her, and, anyway, she wouldn't know how to keep
the office work running smoothly. There were a hundred
different jobs to do. It wasn't just a matter of answering
the phone, opening the mail and making coffee. Helen
West would be able to do that. No doubt Helen West
would enjoy keeping Sam happy, too, but not in the
office. Her idea of making Sam happy would require a
bed.

'Thank you for coming,' she told Mrs Erskine. 'It was
nice to see you, and thank you for the books. I can't
wait to read them both.'

Her mother said, 'I'll walk out with you,' to Sam's
mother, and the two of them went off together, talking
nineteen to the dozen. They were already getting on like
a house on fire. They were very similar types, Natalie
thought, watching them go. They had a lot in common.

She hoped desperately that Mrs Erskine would say
nothing to her mother about that brief, phoney engagement—or had they already talked before they came out
here this morning? She closed her eyes, groaning to herself. Yes, they probably had—and not just about the en-

gagement. They had discussed her and Sam from all angles, shared suspicions and drawn conclusions.

They had had a conspiratorial air every time they looked at each other, now she came to think about it, and all that talk about Sam as a little boy, about grandchildren, betrayed what they had both been thinking. Under the surface of their apparently inconsequential chat they had been making plans, sharing dreams, looking into a future which was never going to happen!

As his mother had said, Sam did not need her—well, she was going to have to talk herself somehow into not needing Sam.

After lunch that Saturday her parents drove to the nearest market town to do some shopping, leaving Natalie in the garden. The sun was so hot she had moved her lounger into the shade of a sycamore. Lying prone, she could gaze up at the gently moving green leaves; light flickered down through them and made dark patterns on her skin. She was wearing shorts and a cutaway cotton top which left her midriff bare. Lazily she moved her legs and admired the shifting leaf-pattern on her thighs for a while until her eyes grew heavy and closed.

She was almost asleep when she heard someone walking fast across the garden, footsteps on the gravel path, angry breathing. Drowsily Natalie lifted her head, and a second later was wide awake, every pulse in her body clamouring with fierce awareness. It was Sam. She took in everything about him with riveted attention: the blue jeans that closely moulded his strong thighs and lean hips, the open-necked white shirt which revealed his tanned throat, the windblown black hair, that mesmerising height, the force of his features.

Alarmed, she also took in the rage glittering in his face. By the time he reached her she was sitting up defensively. Now what? she thought. She had never seen him look so violent. What had put him in this mood?

'I just had a phone call from my mother,' he curtly said. 'How did she get the impression that you and I were living together?'

Natalie turned scarlet, drawing a sharp breath in shock. 'I've no idea!' How on earth had Mrs Erskine picked up such a notion?

Dazedly, Natalie tried to think, but she was confused by having Sam so close to her; his very presence seemed to addle her brains. Her nostrils quivered from the male scent of his tense body; his anger was like smoke on the air. Even when she wasn't looking directly at him she could see him from the corner of her eye, aware of his tiniest movement, of exactly where he was at every second, what he was doing, how he looked, and her aroused senses undermined her ability to think. She couldn't believe that only a few months ago she had been clear-headed and cool in his company.

'No? Who else would have any motive for making up a lie like that?'

CHAPTER EIGHT

'How did you get here?' she asked, looking at the house but not seeing anyone looking back at her. The door leading into the kitchen remained firmly shut and there was no sign of life. 'Did my parents let you in?'

'No—nobody answered when I rang the bell, so I climbed over the gate at the side of the house. And don't try to change the subject. I asked you a question and you're damned well going to answer me. Why did you tell my mother we were living together?'

'I didn't! You must have misunderstood what she said! She was here this morning, for an hour or so, to visit me, and she never said a word to me.'

'I know she was here,' Sam bit out. 'She told me she had seen you.' His face changed, a frown pulling his brows together. 'She said you were still ill. She thought you looked frail.' The grey eyes raked over her, missing nothing of her slender body in the brief shorts and even briefer suntop which left so much of her on view. Immediately she felt hot, as if his eyes burned her.

'Yes, I can see you've lost some weight. I suppose you haven't been eating.' His voice took on a harsher note, but why should he get so furious because she didn't eat? What had it got to do with him? 'I thought your mother would take care of you if you came to stay with her,' he added brusquely. 'Why on earth doesn't she make sure you eat properly?'

'I haven't been hungry most of the time. When you aren't well you don't want to eat!' She was indignant, turning resentful blue eyes on him. Who did he think he

139

was, criticizing her mother like that? 'And she's been wonderful—she's taken a lot of trouble to cook the food I like. She's a great cook; it wasn't her fault I'd lost my appetite.'

'Don't they say that you lose your appetite when you're in love?' Sam drawled, watching her through those narrowed, ice-flecked grey eyes. She hated that look; it made her want to cry. 'Is that why you haven't been eating? Too busy daydreaming over Linklater?'

'I lost my appetite because I'm not well! No other reason! There's nothing going on between me and Johnny! How many times do I have to tell you that?'

She met his eyes and hoped her face didn't betray her. At least he hadn't guessed the truth, that it was him who had taken away her appetite. She would rather die than have Sam know she wasn't eating because she was lovestruck. She despised herself for feeling that way about him. Only schoolgirls constantly daydreamed about a man. It had never happened to her before. She had several times thought she might be in love, but she knew that this time was very different. This time it mattered so much she couldn't think about anything else; waking or asleep, Sam was in the forefront of her mind night and day.

'No?' he derisively enquired, mouth crooked. 'Then why does he keep playing music for you? Do you think I don't know what goes out from my own station? Even if I hadn't heard the programme, and I've been listening all week, I'd have heard all the gossip about the fact that he's been sending you messages.' He grimaced in disgust. '"For a spotty friend!" Good God, what next?'

Why had he been listening? she wondered. He was always too busy to listen to the programmes going out, unless there was something special he wanted to hear. Lately he seemed hostile to Johnny, who had always been one of the station's biggest attractions—was Sam thinking of dumping Johnny's show? Surely not. Johnny still pulled in a huge audience; the figures had dipped slightly over the last couple of months but then listening figures always dipped in summer, when people were out and about more during the fine weather.

'You heard that? I thought it was quite funny.' She shrugged defiantly.

'Then you have the same childish sense of humour Linklater has! You do realise that you two are the hottest item of gossip at work? Everyone's talking about you both. Oh, they don't come out with it to me, and if I'm in earshot they lower their voices, but I get the drift of what they're saying. I've picked up your name being whispered around, coupled with Linklater's, and their faces are a give-away. I can feel them staring after me as I walk past.'

Flushed, she snapped, 'Johnny plays music for nurses at the hospital. Nobody supposes he's having an affair with any of them!'

'He doesn't know them. He doesn't bring them red roses! Has he brought you any more? I suppose he's been visiting you every day since you've been staying here?'

'No, he hasn't! And he hasn't sent me any more flowers, either! How many more times do I have to tell you? I am not dating Johnny!'

'I'm glad to hear you have that much sense. He isn't the marrying kind.'

'Not many men are, these days,' Natalie muttered. She knew Sam wasn't; he had openly said so many times. That was one reason why she had been so stunned when he'd proposed to her at Johnny's party—and why it had seemed such a good joke to pretend she had taken him seriously and believed they really were engaged.

'It's an outdated institution.' Sam shrugged, his face cynical. 'Women keep demanding equality—in jobs, in pay, in opportunities. But marry one of them and in five minutes flat she's divorcing you and claiming half of everything you've worked for all your adult life.'

'That's a bit exaggerated, isn't it?' she protested, resenting the cynicism about her sex.

'All too common these days,' Sam snapped. 'A friend of mine is living in a tiny flat while his wife and child live in the five-bedroomed house he paid a fortune for, and he's still paying her a huge sum every month in alimony. She spends more on clothes than he does on food!'

'As I don't know her I'm not passing judgement on her, but even if what you say is true she's the exception. What about all the mothers having to work, look after their kids, feed them and run the home on a shoestring, because their husbands have deserted them and aren't paying them a penny? I'm prepared to bet there are a lot more of them than there are women who do okay out of a divorce.'

'All the same, I don't give the institution of marriage much of a future.' Sam shrugged again.

She watched him with a heavy heart. Why was he so against marriage? His background didn't give her any clues. His mother was a darling, and seemed to have been very happy with her husband.

'Don't you want children, Sam?' she asked bleakly, and saw his face tighten.

'One day, maybe—but the fact is, one in every three marriages these days ends in divorce, which must cause a lot of problems for the children involved.'

'Sam, if one in three marriages break down, it also means that two out of every three marriages work!' she retorted. He was always claiming to be logical—but he certainly wasn't using logic about marriage, was he?

He laughed abruptly. 'Trust you to look at it that way! Well, even so, marriage is very expensive; a wife always wants a nice home and children, she gives up work and suddenly you're mortgaged to the hilt. I already have too many expenses. My mother's pension from the army doesn't cover much—I have to supplement it—and then there are the girls, Jeanie and Marie. They're both still in full-time education. Oh, they get grants, but it doesn't cover their living costs or buy them clothes, even if they mostly live in jeans and T-shirts. As Jeanie says, a girl has to have at least one pretty dress! My salary is pretty high, thank heavens, but I have to pare my own expenses to the bone to cope with all the demands on me. I certainly couldn't afford to add a wife and kids.'

She looked up at the shifting, sun-dappled leaves of the tree above them, thinking hard. She had always known he was a man who cared deeply about his family, but she had had no idea that he actually supported his mother and sisters to such an extent.

Slowly, she said, 'Yet your mother seems to want you to marry—doesn't she realise what a drain on you she and your sisters are?'

His voice roughened and he frowned. 'No, and I don't want her to know! I deal with all her bills. She writes cheques without any idea how much money she has to cover it. Oh, she's never extravagant—don't get the wrong idea. She's very careful with money, in fact—it's just that the cost of living is so much higher now. She simply doesn't realise how little money she actually has! That house eats money, for instance.'

Natalie was puzzled. 'Oh, does she rent it? I had the idea she owned it.'

'I own it,' he said shortly. 'I bought it some years

ago—not for myself, but for my mother and sisters to live in; they needed a real home, somewhere peaceful in the country. My father was in the army and for years we lived in barracks, both here in the UK and abroad. My mother longed for a home of her own all that time. We lived in rented accommodation after my father died, but as soon as I could afford it I bought that place for them. I'm still paying off the mortgage and I've just had the exterior painted and it cost a fortune—but she's happy there. I don't want her to sell it and move into some pokey little flat.'

'Oh, no, that would be awful!' agreed Natalie, thinking of Mrs Erskine's beautiful home. 'She'd be so miserable!'

'Of course, Jeanie and Marie will be self-supporting in a couple of years, and that will ease the pressure on my bank balance,' Sam added, then suddenly scowled at her. 'Why are we talking about my problems, anyway? We were talking about Linklater; stop trying to change the subject! It's ironic that my own mother has somehow got it into her head that I'm the guy in your life!'

'If you hadn't got drunk at Johnny's party...' she inserted, and got another scowl.

'Yes, okay, we've had all that! Maybe that did start her thinking there was something between you and me—but she didn't get the idea that we were living together from me!'

'I wonder where she did get it?' mused Natalie, trying to think but finding it hard with Sam there. He seemed to have a worrying influence on her ability to think rationally. When they were alone all she could think about was him.

'Oh, come on, Natalie! She must have got it from you! I talked to her yesterday and she didn't mention it then, so she must have picked up this idea some time today. And if not from you, then who?' Frowning, he glanced at the bungalow. 'It wouldn't have been something your parents said, would it? Where are they, by the way?'

'Out shopping—and it can't be my parents who said anything. If they even suspected anything of the sort I'd be the first to hear what they had to say!' She shuddered at the very idea of their reaction. 'They're rather old-fashioned. They wouldn't be too happy to hear I was living with you, and they…well, my mother, anyway… would have a lot to say, believe me.'

'I'm not too happy to hear about it myself!' His voice was scathing, his eyes savage, and she flinched away from his anger. Did he really believe she had started this rumour? That she wanted people to think they were sleeping together?

During the three years they had worked together Sam had made a pass at her from time to time, but it had been an automatic reflex because she was free and available. She knew he had never meant it seriously; she had never taken it seriously.

Some girls she worked with took a pass as an insult, and with some men it might well be—but not if the man was as attractive as Sam, and not if you fancied him, too, and would give anything to believe he actually cared about you. It had been a struggle to turn him down. She wished she took sex as lightly as he apparently did, but she didn't. It wasn't just sex she wanted—sex was always easy to come by if you didn't look like the back of a horse. It was love Natalie needed, and that was something that wasn't on offer from Sam.

Sam was a highly sexed male animal. With him sexual attraction was like hunger—the instant he felt it he tried to satisfy it. But he hadn't pushed it beyond civilised limits. She had said no, so Sam had shrugged without turning nasty and probably gone elsewhere. The idea of him with someone else hurt, but it would have hurt even more to go to bed with a man who only wanted sex from her.

Her voice husky with pain, she said, 'Why didn't you ask your mother why on earth she thinks we're living together?'

'Of course I asked her! But she refused to say—which is why it has to be you. She wouldn't have been so reluctant to name her source otherwise.'

Natalie had been thinking hard; suddenly light dawned. 'Johnny!' she burst out, and Sam stared down at her, his brows heavy.

'What?'

'Remember last week, when you went to collect my pills and Johnny dropped in to see me? You let yourself back in with my front door key. I remember Johnny's expression! He instantly jumped to conclusions and decided we were having an affair.'

'I remember,' Sam slowly said. 'The trouble is, my mother can't have seen Johnny today—he's in London for some big party. Social event of the year, according to him—everyone who's anyone in the music biz is going to be there.'

'Johnny could have passed on gossip about us,' she thought aloud. 'In fact, he'd be bound to! Johnny can't keep a secret—especially if it's somebody else's secret. You said yourself you had picked up the fact that there was a lot of gossip going around. So anyone from the company could have told your mother!'

Sam looked even angrier. 'Oh, that's wonderful! We'll be reading about it in the national press any minute! Well, get this, Natalie, and get it good! We aren't going to be living together, married or unmarried.' He bent, glaring at her, face flushed and tense. 'I know where that would lead—to you blackmailing me, or rail-roading me into marriage. Get it into your head—I am not up for a permanent relationship with anyone. So, you can just ring my mother and tell her we aren't living together, that the idea is a joke—like the joke about us being engaged!'

'Listen, damn you!' Natalie erupted, shaking with fury at what he had just said. 'I did not tell your mother!'

'Okay, okay,' he snarled. 'Have it your way. But you'll still ring her and set the record straight, do you hear?'

'I'd have to be deaf not to! And I'll ring your mother, don't worry! You don't think I want her...want any-one...to believe we're sleeping together, do you? I wouldn't sleep with you if you paid me a million a night!'

His eyes flashed and his face hardened into a savage, angry mask. She saw it with intense satisfaction—so, she had stung his ego, had she? Well, good! He deserved it.

A second later her nerves leapt as Sam angrily bent down and caught hold of her shoulders, his fingers dig-ging into her flesh.

'Get your hands off me!' Natalie snapped, trying to slap his hands away.

Sam ignored her, pulling her up out of the lounger. Dizzily she looked up at him, eyes dark blue with pain and anger.

'Don't you d—' she began, and then his head de-scended and his mouth hit hers with scorching insist-ence, stopping the rest of her sentence and almost suf-focating her.

Her body had been smouldering with passion ever since he'd walked towards her over the grass. Now it burst into fire. She had been dreaming about him for days, aching with frustration and a desire that had been growing deeper and more painful roots with every hour they were apart.

Suddenly the dreams became reality, and she forgot her anger and her resentment. Groaning, she curved into him, one hand clutching his shirt, her mouth parted, hungrily feeding on his kiss, her other arm going round his neck, her hand splayed across his nape, her fingers twining into his thick, dark hair, which clung to her skin. Her palm pushed down on the tense muscles of his neck to bring his head down even closer. She could never get close enough to him; she wanted so desperately to have him inside her, part of her. Perspiration sprang out on her skin; heat burned between her thighs.

Sam's hands were moving, too, one slowly moving back from her back to her bare midriff, inserting itself under her brief top, his fingers cool on her hot skin, stroking upwards until he touched her bare breasts.

She heard the startled intake of his breath as he realised she hadn't bothered to put on a bra today, not having expected visitors. She had forgotten the fact herself, until Sam touched her breast and sent shudders of pleasure through her whole body.

He cupped the soft, full weight of her breast, his fingers caressing her hard nipple, making it swell with aroused blood, and she moaned with pleasure. Sam's mouth lifted from hers. His head came up and she felt him looking at her but kept her eyes shut, afraid he would see in her dilated pupils the reflection of her desire.

She knew she should stop him now; this was crazy, she would hate herself later for letting him do this to her, but at that instant she didn't care. She was dominated by passion. It didn't even enter her head that anyone might see them, or that her parents might come back at any minute.

Luckily the bungalow was isolated; there were no neighbours to peer out of a window or over the high hedge, and nobody walking past could see into the garden, but it would have made no difference to Natalie if there had been witnesses.

Desire had burnt away all her inhibitions—all she knew or cared about at that second was that Sam was making love to her. If the sky fell in, if the world went up in flames, it wouldn't matter to her.

He pulled the long ties which held her top in place and a second later she was naked except for her shorts. Sam bent his head again; his moist tongue moved across her nipple and she arched backwards, almost whimpering, holding his back, feeling his muscles under her fingers clench as he closed his mouth around her nipple and softly sucked it into that moist heat.

'Sam...oh, God...Sam...' she moaned, her hands clutching his supple, powerful back, moving down caressingly to curve over his buttocks, pushing him into her own body, yearning to have him deep inside her, part of her. She needed him so badly; for a long time she had felt incomplete without him.

'You want me!' he whispered hoarsely, burying his face between the full, aching weight of her breasts, his lips moving down the deep valley of warm white flesh. 'Admit it, Natalie. Tell me you want me. I have to hear you say it.'

Eyes shut, she groaned his name again, slipping a hand inside his jeans, and felt with a jagged thrust of pleasure the furnace heat coming from his thighs.

She didn't need to ask if Sam wanted her. His body told her without needing words. If he had wanted to, he couldn't have hidden his desire from her.

Sam shuddered. 'Yes... God, Natalie...touch me...I

want you so badly. I've been going crazy for the past couple of weeks, just thinking about having you.'

With feverish urgency he unzipped her shorts; she felt them slipping down to the ground, leaving her naked except for her tiny silk panties, and made no effort to stop Sam.

Breathing thickly, audibly, Sam grasped one of her thighs, lifted her leg, curled it around his waist and slowly slid his fingers down the smooth white flesh of her inner thigh while with the other hand he unzipped his jeans, allowing his hot, engorged flesh to spring out and brush against her.

She cried out, her body arching in shock and fever, barely able to breathe. Suddenly there was nothing between their naked bodies; the rough hair between his thighs prickled against her sensitive skin and Sam stroked her inner flesh with slow sensuality, his eyes shut, his mouth on her throat.

The summer air hung still and hot around them; it might have been a tropical night for all Natalie knew or cared. Eyes shut, she was blind to the sunlight, deaf to the call of birds. The wild responses of her body dominated her. She wanted Sam too much to stop him now. The moist heat between her thighs waited for him to enter her; she clutched at his buttocks, pushing him towards it, mindless with clamouring desire.

When the hot silence was broken by the sound of a car's engine coming closer they froze, the fierce excitement of passion dying as if someone had chucked cold water over them.

The engine cut out, there was the slam of car doors at the front of the bungalow.

'What the hell?' Sam sounded dazed and she knew how he felt; she was in the same confused and distracted state.

'Oh…God…my parents…' she whispered, her eyes wide again now, blinking, half-blinded by the sunlight. 'They're back!'

Sam swore. Violently. He let go of her, almost pushed her away, with such force that Natalie nearly fell over. Sam turned his back on her and began hurriedly pushing his shirt back into his jeans, zipping them up.

Pulling herself together, Natalie shakily dressed herself too, in such a hurry that her head almost spun. It would be a miracle if her mother didn't notice the state she was in! She ran her fingers through her dishevelled hair but could do nothing about her face, which was burning with embarrassment and shame.

'I can't make polite small talk; I'm not in the mood,' Sam muttered without looking at her. 'I'll leave the way I came.' He paused, then added curtly, 'Ring my mother today. Tell her the truth—we aren't living together and we are not getting married! And don't forget!'

He was gone a second later, striding across the garden to the side of the house, his long black shadow flying ahead of him on the smooth green turf. Natalie watched him vault the locked gate, then he was gone. And a moment later she heard a car engine start up and knew he was driving away.

She hoped to God her parents hadn't spotted him! They would be full of questions if they had, like, Why hadn't he left through the house? And why had he been in such a hurry to get away without being seen?

Legs shaky, her face white now, all the hot blood drained out of her, hating herself and hating Sam, Natalie stumbled to the lounger and lay down, fighting self-contempt. Why had she let him go so far?

She should have hit him the instant he touched her, but she hadn't; within a couple of minutes of telling him she wouldn't sleep with him if he paid her a million a night she had been moaning ecstatically in his arms. She hadn't stopped him undressing her. She hadn't struggled or protested at anything he did. No, on the contrary—she had touched him, too, in a way that had made it all too clear she wanted him. If her parents hadn't come back at that instant, right now she and Sam would be making love.

No! she thought, sickened. Not making love. Sam didn't love her. He just wanted to have sex with her, and she couldn't even pretend she hadn't wanted it too.

Her stomach churned and heaved as she remembered those moments of feverish urgency, her own wild pleasure, the way she had touched him, her aching desire to have him deep inside her. For God's sake—she might just as well have begged him to take her.

She had been out of her mind with passion—but that was no excuse. How could she have let him get so far, so fast, without even once trying to stop him? Where was her self-respect? Well, she had betrayed herself to him now. Sam knew that he could get to her that way, and he was never going to give her any peace until he had had her in bed. And she no longer had any confidence in her own ability to keep him at arm's length.

If she didn't get away from Sam very soon she was going to end up getting badly hurt.

Her mother came down the garden path a few moments later, but Natalie kept her eyes shut and pretended to be asleep. She couldn't face talking to her mother; she was afraid she might give away too much. Her mother knew her too well, could read her face, her voice, like a book. She might not guess what was behind Natalie's mood, but, like a dentist, she would keep probing away until she hit the cause of the symptoms, and Natalie dreaded the idea of her mother knowing she was in love with Sam.

Mrs Craig hesitated, stood there watching her for a moment while Natalie fought to keep her breathing slow and calm, in the sleep pattern, struggled to keep all expression from her face.

She must have succeeded, because after a pause Mrs Craig tiptoed away, leaving Natalie to misery and guilt.

That evening, dry-mouthed and nervous, Natalie rang Mrs Erskine, and without waiting launched at once into what she had to say.

'Sam tells me you seem to have got the idea that we…we're—' At that point she broke off, biting her lip, not knowing quite how to put it.

'Living together?' prompted Mrs Erskine, not sounding as shocked as Natalie had supposed she would. 'Well, yes, Natalie, that's the latest gossip I heard. But Sam tells me it isn't true! I suppose he asked you to ring me and back him up?'

'Er…yes… It really isn't true, Mrs Erskine! I don't know where on earth this gossip came from, but…'

'Helen West.'

Natalie took a furious breath, going red with temper. 'Oh, so it was her? I might have guessed!'

'Hell hath no fury,' agreed Mrs Erskine. 'She's livid because Sam and she have split up. I must say I was very relieved to hear it. I never thought much of her— all make-up and no manners.'

Natalie liked Mrs Erskine more and more.

Mrs Erskine added, 'That's why I wasn't exactly delighted to meet her on my way back from visiting you. I stopped to do some shopping and ran into Helen. I could see at once that she was in a spiteful temper. She's one of those catty girls who love to use their claws on you even though you haven't done anything to them.'

'Yes, isn't she?' Natalie agreed fervently. 'That's a very shrewd description of her.'

'I would have preferred to pretend I didn't remember her, but one has to be polite, so I said hello and asked how she was, and all I got was pure poison. She almost spat at me: did I know Sam was living with you and everyone was talking about it? She said a few other things about you that I won't repeat. I suppose she expected me to faint in shock or be embarrassed, but I was so cross I just said, So what? and walked off, although I must admit I was taken aback. But I wouldn't give that woman the satisfaction of seeing I was stunned.'

'Good for you,' Natalie said. 'What other things did she say about me? Don't worry, I won't faint if you tell me. I know she hates the sight of me.'

'Yes, I gathered that—interesting, isn't it? I wonder why she's so poisonous about you?'

'What did she say?' repeated Natalie.

'Well, my dear, are you sure you want to hear such unpleasant comments?'

'I like to know what's being said about me behind my back! No doubt she's said it to others, if she said it to you.'

Mrs Erskine sighed. 'Probably, but I'm sure everyone will see what a pack of lies it is!'

'I hope they will, but I'd still like to know exactly what she's saying!'

Reluctantly his mother said, 'Well, she says you've been chasing Sam ever since you started working for him.'

'Oh, does she?' Natalie couldn't help bursting out, hot-cheeked and indignant. Chasing Sam indeed! 'I did nothing of the kind!'

'Of course you wouldn't, Natalie—and, knowing my son, he'd run a mile from any woman who did chase him. You know, I always swore I'd welcome any girl Sam brought home, but when I met Helen West my heart sank at the very idea of Sam marrying someone like her. Thank God he had more sense!'

Natalie didn't comment on how much sense Sam had; she didn't want to upset his mother by being too frank about her son's mental processes.

'What else did she say?' she pressed, and heard his mother sigh.

'Oh, well…more nonsense! She said you trapped Sam into an affair. As if I'd believe a fairy tale like that. I know it isn't true, any of it—absolute nonsense—nobody who knows you could possibly doubt that, Natalie.'

'It is nonsense,' Natalie flatly told her. 'Believe me, Sam was telling the truth…we aren't living together or having an affair. So, please forget everything she told you!'

'Of course I will, but I can't help hoping it isn't all moonshine—well, not the part about you and Sam getting together at last. I'm so sick of waiting for him to settle down and start a family. I sometimes think I'll be pushing up the daisies before Sam gives me a grandchild. If you could see your way to turning a blind eye to all his faults I'd be very grateful!'

Huskily Natalie laughed. 'He wouldn't be very pleased if he heard this conversation!'

'I won't tell him, if you won't!'

'You're very naughty,' Natalie said, amused and touched. She was glad his mother liked her; it was mutual, but at the same time it made her own situation far more painful.

'When you're better you must come over and paint with me again,' his mother said. 'I enjoyed that afternoon—I hope you did, even if you were coming down with measles. I suppose that was why you left so hurriedly? You felt ill?'

'Yes,' Natalie hedged, knowing it was half a lie. She

had felt very odd that afternoon, but she couldn't now remember whether her feverish state had been due to Sam or to the onset of measles. 'I had a wonderful time; I'd love to do it again.'

'Soon, I hope,' Mrs Erskine said.

Natalie was making the phone call from her bedroom, and suddenly heard footsteps outside her door.

'Yes, soon—well, I have to go now. Goodbye, Mrs Erskine,' she hurriedly said, and put the phone down just as her mother came into the room with a mug of hot chocolate.

'I'm sorry, I didn't know you were on the phone,' Mrs Craig said, looking at her shrewdly, curiosity in her eyes.

'Natalie accepted the mug being held out to her. 'Mmm…this smells wonderful!' Casually she added, 'I was talking to Mrs Erskine—she invited me to spend an afternoon painting at her house when I'm better.'

Her mother's face brightened. 'How kind of her. It's nice that you two share a hobby; it makes such a bond. I was saying to your father this morning that we ought to invite her and Sam to dinner one evening—I'd like to get to know both of them better.'

Natalie heard all the things her mother wasn't saying—the questions, the eagerness, the veiled curiosity. Her face tight, she said in a voice she tried to make flat and unrevealing, 'Maybe one day, when I'm really well again, but not yet, Mum.'

'No, probably wiser to wait a while.' Mrs Craig nodded.

When she had left again Natalie sat, nursing her hot chocolate, so eaten up by pain and anger that she couldn't move for a while. What was she going to do? She couldn't face anyone at work, knowing what they were thinking, if not saying, and she couldn't face Sam again, either, remembering those moments in the sunlit garden.

She had to get away from him before he broke her heart. She shut her eyes, flinching. Oh, don't be so melodramatic! she scolded herself. Hearts don't break. Oh, no? she thought. Then why does my heart hurt so much? If it isn't breaking, what the hell is wrong with it?

I'm having a heart attack, that's all. It isn't fatal, and there is no use going to see a cardiac specialist. This isn't a pain that would show up on their electronic equipment; you can't hear or see it. But she had had enough. There was a limit to how much anguish you could bear, and she had reached it.

CHAPTER NINE

SHE didn't tell her parents what she planned to do because she knew only too well how her mother would react. Mrs Craig was so eager for her and Sam to get together that she would be horrified—she would ask endless questions, would probe and protest, until Natalie went crazy. The best thing would be to write to her parents once she had gone—it would be easier to tell them in a letter, rather than face to face. The same applied to Sam, of course—even more so!

It might be cowardly but Natalie didn't feel strong enough to do it any other way. Discretion was the better part of valour, especially where Sam was concerned.

Her father drove her back to her flat a week later, and left her there. She stood at the window of her flat, grey with misery in spite of the marvellous morning sunshine. The view had never looked lovelier—the sea had a blue dancing glitter, the sky was full of gulls like scraps of white paper blown across the horizon, and the little town stretched below, the buildings all shapes and sizes and colours, red roofs, pastel-painted walls, the shabby elegance of old hotels and a crescent of Georgian town houses, the modern white blocks of flats set in billiard-table-smooth green lawns.

Natalie had often enjoyed painting that view. She hated leaving it; she hated the idea of not waking up to the sound of gulls and the fresh wind from the sea. She had always loved living close to both sea and countryside. She didn't want to move up to noisy, dirty, busy London; she hated cities. Whenever she had visited one she had felt alienated. There were too many people, too much traffic, a bewildering maze of streets going on and on for ever.

But she couldn't see any alternative. Sam had her pinned like a mouse in a corner; her only chance of escape was to run while he wasn't looking.

Now that he knew his power over her he would never give up; it wasn't in the nature of the beast to let a trapped victim get away, and Natalie couldn't face the thought of having a brief affair with him and then watching him walk away from her, as he had from every other girlfriend he had had since she met him.

Only a masochist would deliberately get into a relationship that could only end in pain, and Natalie was no masochist. She wouldn't be able to stop loving him just because she no longer saw him, of course. She was too much of a realist to hope for that. But surely her feelings would gradually ebb away? Love could be starved to death. Couldn't it? Her face set bleakly. She would make sure of that. She wouldn't even let herself think about Sam from now on.

Sighing, she turned away from the window. What she should be doing was some packing; she would only take a couple of suitcases—she would get her mother to pack up the rest of her things later.

She put two cases on her bed and began to hunt through her wardrobe, trying to decide what to take and what to leave. Two minutes later, someone rang the doorbell.

Sam! she instantly thought, so shocked that she let go of a pair of heavy black riding boots she was holding. They hit a chair which was already overburdened with objects and knocked it over. The resulting crash seemed to reverberate through the whole building.

For a moment afterwards there was silence, then the

doorbell rang again, far louder. Whoever was outside must have heard the chair fall over; there was no point in pretending she wasn't in! Heart banging inside her chest, Natalie opened the door. But it wasn't Sam, it was Johnny, his supple body graceful in tight white jeans and a cut-off black cotton top which showed his smooth, tanned midriff.

He gave her one of his slow, charming smiles. 'Hello, long time no see! Glad you're back. I was driving past half an hour ago when I saw you getting out of a car. I'd have stopped to chat then, but I'd promised to drop off some discs to a fan; she's an old darling, eighty years old, blind and bedridden. Listens to the radio all day, rings me up once a week on air, and is always good value. My public love her, and so do I.'

He had a soft heart hidden somewhere under all that little-boy charm, but he kept it out of sight most of the time—which was probably very wise as some people would take advantage of him if they knew.

'That was nice of you, Johnny.'

He grimaced, shrugging the compliment away. 'Not at all. She's doing me a favour—I get so many discs and tapes sent to me by record companies that if I kept them all I wouldn't have room to move in my flat. So every couple of months I drive round to Fanny with a box full. Her next door neighbour has the key to Fanny's place; I let her know I'm coming and she makes a pot of tea and lets me in. I spend half an hour with Fanny and we have a cup of tea together. She's a lively old dear; I enjoy talking to her.' He looked past Natalie, quirking an eyebrow quizzically. 'Going to ask me in? Or have you got a visitor? I saw the guy driving the car—was that your father, or have you developed a taste for much older men?'

She laughed. 'Idiot! It was my father; he simply dropped me here and went.'

'What a relief! How are you? Better now? Spots all gone?' He studied her thoughtfully. 'No spots in sight—but you're very pale, and you look depressed, sweetheart. What you need is some TLC.'

Blankly she repeated, 'TLC?'

'Tender loving care, which is what I'm here to give you—are you going to let me in or not?'

She sighed, standing back, and he sauntered past. Closing the front door, Natalie cursed her luck. Why had Johnny been driving past at just that moment? She looked round and found him staring down at her open cases and the clothes piled on her bed.

'What's going on?' He shot a shrewd glance at her. 'Are you packing or unpacking? Looks to me as if you're packing—you've just been away for a couple of weeks. Going away again so soon?'

Hurriedly, she pleaded, 'Don't tell anyone, Johnny. I'll be writing, but I don't want anyone to know I'm going until he gets my letter.'

'By he you mean Sam?' interpreted Johnny, eyes narrowed. 'You're dumping him?'

'No... I... The thing is...' Her mind was in a pathetic state of confusion; she could only stammer, breaking down at last into a wail. 'Oh, you don't understand! Look, just promise you won't say a word. And this time swear it...or I'll never forgive you!' She looked at him reproachfully. 'I know it was you who told everyone Sam had a key to my place, that we were living together. It had to be you, so don't deny it. You upset his mother...'

Flushing, Johnny protested, 'I never said a word to his mother!'

'No, but Helen West did!'

He groaned. 'She didn't? What a nasty piece of work that woman is!'

Natalie wasn't arguing with that. 'Yes, that's what she

is, all right, but she could only repeat the story because you talked after you'd promised me you wouldn't. You caused me a lot of embarrassment, Johnny.'

Shamefaced, he muttered, 'Sorry, Nat,' looking down. 'I only mentioned it to a couple of people!'

'Couple of hundred, you mean!' she scornfully retorted. 'I know you're a natural broadcaster, but keep other people's private lives to yourself, for God's sake, Johnny. You can do a lot of harm by spreading stories like that.' Her blue eyes flashed with threat. 'If I find out you've told anyone I was leaving, before tomorrow lunchtime, I promise you I'll come back and find you—and I swear I'll make you sorry, Johnny.'

Hurriedly, he promised. 'I won't breathe a syllable! I swear it, by everything holy…Elvis, Buddy Holly, Marilyn…all my dead saints!'

She couldn't help laughing at that, but sobered a second later. 'I hope you're serious! Because I am. If you break your word I'll be back, and I'll tell everyone how old you'll be next birthday.'

Johnny went pale. 'There's no need to be that vindictive! I was just going to ask you out to lunch somewhere really special, too! I've made a booking at Les Tourterelles—you know it? French restaurant high on the cliffs, outside town, opened only a couple of months ago and already you need to book weeks in advance to get a good table.'

She was impressed, and tempted. She had heard people talking about Les Tourterelles; the restaurant was the 'in' place for lovers at the moment, which was obviously the intention of the owner or why would he have called it The Turtledoves?

Johnny gave her a coaxing smile. 'You'd love it. The food is fabulous and the setting is perfect, especially in summer. It will cheer you up.'

Well, why not? There was no hurry for her to finish packing this morning—she had all day—and she *was* depressed; he was right. She needed something special to lift her spirits.

'Just give me two minutes to get ready!' she conceded, and Johnny grinned, eyes brightening.

'Great. I'll wait outside in the car. I have a couple of phone calls to make on my mobile phone.'

It took a little longer than two minutes. Such a good restaurant warranted something a little better than the old jeans she was wearing, so she changed into one of her favourite summer dresses: glazed cotton, white with a print of soft-washed lavender flowers, the scooped neckline leaving her throat bare, the full skirts swirling around her bare legs when she walked, making satisfying swishing noises. In case the weather changed while she was out she took a white lambswool cardigan with her, too, draping it over her shoulders and letting it hang loose over her arms.

The top of Johnny's sports car was down; his blond head gleamed in the sunlight. As she walked towards him he considered her through the mirror sunglasses shielding his eyes, then leaned over and opened the passenger door for her.

'You look gorgeous!'

She slid into the seat next to him, smiling at him as she closed the car door again and clipped her seat belt. 'So do you!'

'You're a doll.' Johnny grinned, starting the engine and shooting away from the kerb as if he were driving in a race.

'Slow down!' Natalie said breathlessly,. her hair blowing around her face, and as he slotted into the town traffic Johnny obligingly slowed to the speed of the other cars.

The day was warm and sunny, the blue sky cloudless. Les Tourterelles turned out to be a tiny restaurant in what had obviously once been a Victorian farmworker's cottage. Given a choice of tables, Johnny chose one on a patio at the back of the building, with a great view of the sea and cliffs. They ate under a canopy, which gave them some shade, and took their time with the meal, enjoying the ambience as well as the view stretching as far as the eye could see.

Natalie chose Coquilles Saint-Jacques to start with, the local scallops cooked in wine, with tiny whole mushrooms. Johnny had some local crab, in its shell, served with salad, and then they both chose duck breasts served with fresh local asparagus and new potatoes. For dessert they ate strawberries, and finished with the restaurant's excellent coffee.

While they ate Johnny talked about a dozen different subjects—fan mail, a pop concert he had been to in London, the latest top group, scandal in the music business. He was drinking most of the very good white wine he had chosen; Natalie made one glass last a long time.

Towards the end of the meal, Johnny suddenly said, 'What do you think about a new club?'

Bewildered, she asked, 'A club? Which club?'

'Night club—here, in town. Remember we talked about the idea a few times? Well, I'm still thinking of running one—while I'm still hot and the kids know my name I thought, why not open a club? Bit of insurance. Then if… Well, it would be something to fall back on later.'

She understood him then—what Johnny meant was that if his programme ever got taken off the air, owning a night club would be a good insurance policy.

'I'm looking around for partners—expensive business, opening a club. Technical equipment costs a fortune, and then there's the décor; need a good designer for that. I'd need business partners, guys with money to put up. You know what they say—never put your own money into a risky business!'

'I'm sure that's a wise policy,' she agreed.

'In any case, I'd be putting up my name and involved in running the place. I'll call it Johnny's Place, and I mean to be there every night—talk to the customers, spin a few discs. I reckon it would be a goldmine. I have several local businessmen making interested noises about putting up the money.'

'Be careful, Johnny,' she said, wondering how much he knew about business. 'You need advice before you sign anything. Get a lawyer to vet your contracts first, won't you? And make sure you have a good accountant keeping an eye on the books. You don't want to end up with nothing while your partners walk off with all your money.'

'I won't put up my own money,' Johnny said, laughing at her. 'Don't worry about me, honey. I'm smarter than the average bear!'

He drove her back to her flat in the late afternoon, their hair blowing in a little breeze which had got up by then, refreshingly cool after the summer heat earlier.

'Care for some more coffee?' she invited, before getting out of the car.

'Love some,' said Johnny, opening his door and sliding out to open hers. He helped her out with typical gallantry, bending over her as if she were made of porcelain. As Natalie straightened she felt Johnny stiffen, heard the intake of his breath.

'On second thoughts, I think I'd better be on my way,' he abruptly said, and hurried round to his own side of the car again while Natalie stared after him, bemused by his change of mind.

Until she stepped onto the pavement outside her block of flats and saw what had made Johnny run away so fast.

Her heart jolted in shock; she stopped dead in her tracks. Sam stood in the doorway, watching them with the hard, narrowed stare of a streetfighter. His eyes were so cold she shivered in spite of the hot sunlight, and might even have jumped back into Johnny's sports car if he hadn't driven away at that second like a streak of lightning.

But that would be cowardly, so she stiffened her backbone and walked on towards him.

'What are you doing here, Sam?' she asked him, with what she hoped sounded like cool indifference.

'Waiting for you,' he said, standing back to let her pass. He didn't move far out of her way, just enough for her to squeeze past, so that Natalie had to make herself as thin as she could and wriggle by, their bodies an inch or so apart. He was doing it deliberately, she knew that, so she kept her eyes lowered, barely breathing because his closeness affected every part of her, invaded her bloodstream, made her heart beat faster, made her head swim—but she would not let him know that.

Damn him! she thought as she got past and was able to let out her breath. He knew by now what it could do to her to be that close to him. But she restrained her desire to run and walked slowly to her own front door, found her key in her pocket, then turned to face him, chin up.

'I'm busy—can whatever you want to say wait, please?'

She could not let him inside her flat—he would see the cases on her bed, the clothes strewn around, and would start asking questions she did not want him to ask.

'No, it won't,' he said, taking the key out of her hand

and putting it into the lock. The door swung open and, grabbing her elbow, Sam propelled her through the door into her flat.

'What do you think you're doing, pushing me around?' she burst out, desperate to keep him out, trying to block his view of the long studio flat by standing right in front of him while she snatched her key out of his hand. 'Go away, will you?'

For answer, Sam kicked the front door shut and she jumped at the sound; it felt like a door slamming in her head, or in her heart. The echo went on and on, deafening her.

Why did men always resort to temper when they couldn't cope with a situation? Why couldn't they discuss it calmly and rationally? Why did they reach for rage automatically, to express a whole range of deep feelings...jealousy, pain, resentment, even love? Why couldn't they talk to people instead of yelling and stamping about?

What were they so afraid of that their only emotional outlet was to lose their temper?

'The minute you're back in town,' he said through his teeth, bewildering her.

'What?' Had she missed the first part of that sentence? She couldn't think straight with him so close to her, especially when he looked at her that way and spoke in that terse voice.

Her innocent question seemed to inflame him even more. His voice shook with fury. 'The minute you're back in town you're seeing him! Don't lie about it. I know you only got back this morning; my mother rang to tell me.'

'Your mother?' Did everyone else in the world have to keep interfering? This should be just her and Sam alone. Her pulses beat wildly at the thought. Her and Sam. Alone. Oh, stop thinking about it! she told herself with contempt. How was she ever to get over him if her own mind kept coming up with images like that?

Like what? she defended, but she knew. Her mind had come up with a brief, intense image of her and Sam in the garden that day, making love with that wild sensuality. How could she forget the man who shared memories like that?

His mouth twisted angrily. 'She seems to have struck up a warm friendship with your mother. Apparently they talk on the phone all the time. My mother felt I ought to know you were back at your flat. She told me I ought to take you out to lunch.'

Disappointment welled up inside her. If only Sam had got here earlier she could have had lunch with him instead of Johnny!

'I'm sorry…' she began, then stopped as his eyes glittered at her like the points of swords in duel.

'Don't bother to lie, Natalie! I drove round here just in time to see you drive off with Linklater. I suppose you let him know you were coming back, and made a date? I'm only your boss—why would I need to be kept informed about your movements? It would have been time enough for me to find out you were coming back to work when you showed up on Monday!'

His scathing tone had worked her up into such a rage by then that before she could stop herself she had snapped back, 'I won't be!'

Sam froze, staring at her fixedly, his face pale and rigid and his eyes leaping with a feeling that made her wish she hadn't been fool enough to tell him.

'What do you mean?'

'I'm leaving. R-resigning. I've d-decided to move to London.' She tried to sound calm and sure of herself, but her courage ran out of her as she met his eyes. She began to stutter. She had often seen him in a temper, raging and yelling around the office—but she had never seen Sam look as if at any minute he might actually kill someone.

Nervously she backed away from the threat of his proximity, into the room, forgetting that Sam would then have an uninterrupted view of the whole flat, of her bed, the open cases, the strewn belongings which she had been packing earlier.

He took a harsh, audible breath, stared at them, then began breathing roughly, raggedly, as though he had some terrible illness which had drained all the colour from his face and aged him fast. She could suddenly see what Sam would look like when he was old.

'The hell you are!' he said in a voice she didn't recognise—a hoarse, shaking voice that made her stomach turn over in panic. 'You aren't going anywhere! I won't let you.'

'You can't stop me!' she defied, but kept her distance, afraid of letting him get too near her. What was the matter with him? 'Will you please go? I don't want you here.'

Sam's eyes flashed and he took a long stride towards her, saying through his teeth, 'Oh, don't you?'

She couldn't back any further; the wall was right behind her. She was trapped and could only throw back her head in a gesture of defiance, her black hair still windblown after the ride back in Johnny's open-topped car, staring up at Sam without flinching, hoping he couldn't see how nervous she was behind her pretence of assurance.

'No, I don't. I want to finish packing. I'm leaving in the morning.'

'You are not leaving! I won't let you go.' He reached for her and Natalie slid under his outstretched arms and shot towards the door again, pulled it open and stood there, trembling but determined.

'I am going, Sam, and so are you, right now! I've had enough. I never want to see you again.'

Sam stood there rigidly, his back to the window, staring at her, his whole body as taut as a drawn bowstring. His hands were clenched at his sides, she could see the muscles in his neck knotted, and the bones in his face seemed to push through his skin. He was really angry now! she thought, shivering, and looked defiantly into his eyes.

They glittered back at her, wide and wet...

Natalie jerked in shock. Wet? Involuntarily, she took a step closer, staring harder into the grey eyes she had always thought so hard and assured—and she hadn't imagined it.

There were tears in Sam's eyes.

She let go of the front door, which swung shut with a bang. 'Sam?' she whispered, doubting, hoping, afraid to believe the evidence of her own eyes, and put out a hand to him.

He flinched as if the touch of it would burn, and abruptly turned away, stood by the window, his back to her. She saw his shoulders moving.

Sam was crying. Sam! Of all men in the world.

She couldn't bear to see him look like that—tears sprang into her own eyes, blinding her. She ran to him and, a sob in her throat, slid between him and the window, put both arms around his waist and laid her head on his chest—and with incredulity felt it moving with soundless sobs under her cheek.

'Sam...darling...don't...'

For a second she felt the rigidity of his body rejecting her, and wondered if she had imagined those tears, if Sam was, after all, just furious.

He took hold of her to push her away, his long fingers biting into her shoulders, hurting her, and she flung her head back to look up at him, tears running down her face.

'I'm going because I love you, Sam, don't you understand? Are you so blind that you can't see I can't bear to stay and see you every day if you don't love me?'

He still held her, staring down at her as if he were a deaf man and could not hear what she was saying, was trying to read her lip movements.

'What?' His voice was hoarse, unfamiliar.

She had burnt her boats now. She had said it out loud; she couldn't take it back, pretend she had never said it.

Taking her courage in both hands, she said it again. 'I said, I love you. Oh, for heaven's sake, Sam…do you want it in writing? Should I have sent you a fax?'

His throat moved in a convulsive swallow; he moistened his lips as if his mouth was so dry he could hardly speak. 'Natalie…' His voice was so low and husky she only just heard the word. 'Oh, God, Natalie.' His arms went round her then, and held her so tightly she was half suffocating. He put his cheek down on her hair and she felt him shuddering. 'If you knew how I felt! When you said you were going away. I thought I would go mad. It was like dying, the thought of not seeing you.'

He lifted his head and she looked up at him, smiling through her tears, rainbows of happiness in her eyes.

'Tell me…tell me you love me… I said it, Sam… can't you?'

He groaned, bent and kissed her wet eyes, breathed huskily, 'Stop looking at me and I may get the words out.' But then his mouth slid down her cheek and found her lips, and Natalie hungrily kissed him back, her arms winding round his neck and holding him.

She felt his lips shaping the words she couldn't hear

but which beat through her veins like wildfire. 'I love you.'

'Sam...' she breathed, her fingers clenching in his thick, warm hair.

He lifted her up off the floor and carried her over to her bed, laid her down full-length on it and fell down beside her, burying his face in her throat, kissing her warm skin and muttering feverishly.

'Natalie, darling. God, Natalie, I'm crazy about you—out of my head. I have been for months, although I wouldn't admit it. I just kept looking at you and thinking how much I'd love to get you into bed, and feeling sick with frustration because I knew you weren't the type to hop into bed with any guy who asked you.'

Chill feathers swept over her skin—had his tears, the silent confession that he loved her, been nothing but a final attempt to get her into bed?

Unaware of what she was thinking, Sam said thickly, 'When I began to suspect you were having an affair with Johnny Linklater I was so jealous I wanted to kill you—both of you. At first I thought I was just angry for being taken in—I'd believed you'd meant it when you said you didn't sleep around. I have to admit I liked the idea that I wouldn't just be one in a long line of guys who had been in your bed. I know I have a reputation as a bit of a womaniser myself—but the truth is there haven't been that many women. Oh, I've dated quite a few, but with most of them I didn't end up in bed. My reputation was mostly smoke and not much fire. Which was why I was as bitter as hell when I thought you were sleeping with Linklater.' He leaned over her to stare into her face, his eyes searching, dark and intent. 'Tell me the truth. Did you sleep with him, Natalie?'

She looked back at him levelly, her own face very serious, and shook her head. 'No, Sam. Nothing ever happened between me and Johnny. I'm fond of him; he's a good friend. Nothing else.'

Sam let out a long, harsh breath. 'It's been torturing me…thinking about it—the idea of you and him together, in bed, making love. When I realised how much it hurt to imagine you with him, I finally had to face the fact that I didn't just fancy you, I was in love.'

She took his face between her hands, her palms caressing his cheeks, and smiled at him.

'How do you think I've felt about all the other women I've had to see you with over the last three years? You don't need to tell me how jealousy feels. I know every twist of the knife.'

'I was never in love with any of them,' Sam muttered, eyes passionate, undoing the buttons on her dress.

'Not even Helen West?'

He grimaced. 'Certainly not her. I'd only been dating her a short while when she began dropping hints about getting married. I made it clear where I stood on that subject, and from then on it was a running battle. She wouldn't stop talking about it. Remember the night of Linklater's party? Helen flirted with him to try to make me jealous enough to propose. I knew what was in her mind, and I remember thinking she was wasting her time because I just was not the jealous type.'

Natalie frowned. 'Yet you came over and started dancing with me. You even proposed to me!' She sighed. 'Sam, you must have been jealous over Helen and Johnny, or why did you do that?'

He leaned down, pushed back her lacy white bra and kissed her breasts lingeringly. 'Don't you know the saying *in vino veritas*, darling? I was drunk enough to do what I had been thinking about and resisting for months…ask you to marry me. It had nothing to do with Helen. The real irony is that I didn't give a damn whether Helen danced with Johnny, or anyone else. She could have slept with any man there and it wouldn't have mattered to me. But the very idea of anyone but me making love to you drove me crazy. I hadn't had to face that fact before because I hadn't seen you with anyone. It was only when I saw you with Linklater that I realised how I felt.'

She was breathless with happiness, until she remembered what he had just said about marriage, and then her heart sank again.

'Sam…there's just one thing. I don't want to mislead you. I have to tell you this—I'm no different from Helen West, you know. I want to get married, too. Oh, not immediately—I don't mean right away—but one day I want a home and children. I don't just want a love affair. I don't just want you for a few months, or a year—I want you for the rest of my life.'

He smiled at her and opened his mouth to say something, but she put a finger on his lips, hurriedly going on because she had to be honest; she didn't want him claiming later that she hadn't been totally frank with him.

'I'm not equipped to fall in and out of love over and over again, Sam. I'd hate that sort of life. It isn't my scene. I've dated several guys over the past three years, but none of them mattered to me—none of them cared about me, either. So none of them lasted beyond a few weeks. And I didn't sleep with any of them because I knew I could never love them, and I didn't want to wake up one day and start counting all the men I'd slept with but never loved.'

Sam picked up her hand and turned it palm upward, bent his head and kissed the soft pink centre of it very gently.

'I'd hate it if you were that type of girl. I don't want

to be another guy in a long queue of men who've been through your bed. And I want you for my whole life, too, darling. I never thought I'd want to get married, until I realised that I'd kill anyone who tried to take you away from me.'

She ran her fingers through his hair, her lips quivering. 'Nobody could take me away from you. I'm afraid I'm the faithful type. But you never have been, have you, Sam? What I'm afraid of is you leaving me one day. It would break my heart.'

His face was sober, almost sombre, his eyes dark with feeling. 'I'll never leave you; you don't have to worry about that! As to marriage, well, over the past week I've thought long and hard about the future. In a couple of years both my sisters will be off my hands, financially. I'll have far more money then, although I'll still have to take care of my mother.' He looked anxiously at her. 'You understand, don't you, Natalie? When my father died I swore to her I'd always take care of her, and I have to keep that promise.'

'I wouldn't want you to do anything else! I love your mother. Sam, money isn't that important! I have my own flat—I could sell that, you could sell yours, we could buy a house together.'

Eagerly, Sam said, 'Well, that was what I thought. We could buy one of those early Victorian town houses down by the harbour. They're still quite cheap, because most of them need a lot of work—they've been allowed to deteriorate for years. But once they've been modernised and redecorated they will be valuable properties, and it would be very convenient for work.'

Startled, she said drily, 'You really have been thinking about it! You haven't actually offered for one, have you?' It would be just like him to go ahead without even talking to her first!

He grinned. 'No, of course not. We'll look at houses together. And choose the new décor together, and the furniture. It will be fun.' That idea seemed to surprise him. 'It will be,' he slowly said, as if it was Natalie who needed to be persuaded.

'Yes, it will be fun,' she softly said.

Sam gave a deep sigh. 'It's been quite a strain, the last few weeks—all that emotional upheaval. I feel amazingly tired all of a sudden.' He stretched his long body beside her, but he didn't seem tired to her; the air around him vibrated with passion and energy. 'Do you like that dress, by the way?' he asked.

'Yes, I do, or I wouldn't wear it—don't you?' She was puzzled by his question, and a little hurt; she had thought the lavender and white dress suited her.

'I love it,' he assured her. 'It makes your eyes a wonderful dark blue. So I wouldn't want it getting crumpled.' He sat up, pulling her up too. She was bewildered until he whipped her dress up, over her head. A second later Sam tossed it onto a chair nearby and turned back to look at her.

Dry-mouthed, she felt her body shake with fierce excitement. Sam didn't need to tell her what was in his mind. She read it in his eyes, felt the same flaring heat beating inside her.

'I've waited a lifetime to do this,' Sam muttered, sliding the straps of her slip down over her arms.

'So have I,' she whispered, her fingers trembling as she undid his buttons and pulled off his shirt, dropped it on the floor without looking. She buried her face in him, breathing in the scent of his skin, her lips apart, tasting him, while she undid his jeans, feverish with urgency.

Her slip had gone, and her bra; she was only wearing tiny silk panties now. She wanted him naked, too; she ached for his body on top of her, inside her; she needed him part of her; she had to have him buried in her, completing her. Sam kicked off his jeans and the black briefs he wore underneath, and Natalie's blood sang in her ears; she was scarcely able to breathe.

For a few seconds they stared at each other, not touching, their naked bodies so close, yet not close enough.

Natalie slowly ran her hand down his powerful figure, exploring it from his wide shoulders to that deep chest and the short dark hair curling down the centre of it, to his midriff, following his hips, then dipping down to trace the flat abdomen, feeling the rough hair lower down brushing her palm and then, even more slowly, softly, tormenting the hard, hot, swelling flesh below that.

Sam groaned, eyes half-shut, their greyness, bright as moonlight, shimmering through his black lashes. One of his hands cupped her breast; he bent his head and nuzzled it, sucking her nipple into his hot mouth, while his other hand stroked downwards, his fingers sliding between her thighs, forcing a wild cry of pleasure from her as he softly rubbed a finger back and forth, in and out.

A moment later she was on her back and Sam was on top of her, urgent, breathing as if he were dying, pushing her thighs apart and climbing between them. His hands went underneath her, lifting her, opening her, then she felt the fierce thrust of his flesh moving up inside. Head flung back, eyes shut, she moaned ecstatically, then, their arms clasped round each other, they drove on towards the final, shuddering satisfaction they had been waiting for so long.

Afterwards, Sam fell on her, shaking and breathing thickly, and lay with his head pillowed on her breasts while Natalie held him as if he were a baby, stroking his tousled hair, caressing his long, lean back, her fingers tenderly following the deep indentations of his spine.

He was hers. She could touch him when she liked, hold him in her arms every night—she couldn't believe it; she was still incredulous in spite of the intense pleasure he had just given her.

Was she dreaming? Was all this just another dream, like all the dreams she had had of him for so long? Would she wake up in a minute and find herself alone in her bed, in her flat?

Her arms closed even more possessively around his warm, breathing body. No, Sam was here. Sam was real, not a dream, and he belonged to her. Her body was still hot and moist, deep inside, from his lovemaking, her mouth still swollen from his passionate kisses, her breasts still aching from his mouth.

Sam turned his head, yawning, and pushed his lips against her naked breast.

'I could sleep for weeks,' he said drowsily, eyes shut. 'I love you.'

'I love you, Sam,' she whispered.

A moment later she realised he was asleep, his body limp and heavy on her. Natalie shifted to make his weight easier, her arms still round him, his cheek against hers, and let herself drift into half-dream, half-sleep.

CHAPTER TEN

BEFORE they announced their engagement, Sam suggested they should get married first.

'First?' Natalie blinked, puzzled. 'You mean before we...?'

'Instead of,' nodded Sam, and she searched his face uneasily.

'No engagement, in other words? We just...'

'Get married,' he said eagerly. 'Cut out the boring middle stuff. No engagement party, no fuss and planning and getting hassle from the parents. We just get married immediately, and without warning anyone until the last minute. My mother will want the whole rigmarole, Natalie: wedding cakes and bridesmaids and white limousines with white satin ribbons—we don't want that, do we?' His eyes pleaded with her to agree and Natalie had to kiss him because he looked so sweet. Being desperate suited Sam.

'I know what you mean, darling...' Relief filled his face, but she ruthlessly added, 'But we don't want to disappoint our families, do we?'

His face fell again. 'Don't we?'

'Sam, I love your mother, and she's been looking forward to your wedding for so long—we can't cheat her of that, can we? You wouldn't want to make her miserable, would you?'

'No, but...' Sam was very agitated now. 'Natalie, after all, this is our wedding, not hers, and all that stuff is just a lot of show and ritual!'

She considered him ruefully—there was a lot he didn't

know about women, wasn't there? For a man who had had quite a few girlfriends in the past, and who cared so much about his mother and sisters, he was oddly blind about the opposite sex.

In gentle tones she tried to put him in the picture. 'Women feel strongly about rituals, Sam. Surely you've noticed that? It isn't usually men who write Christmas and birthday cards, who buy family presents, arrange family parties—it is nearly always women, because they believe ritual is the cement that holds lives together.'

'Women love being busy, you mean,' Sam cynically informed her. 'That's why it's them who arrange parties and Christmas and stuff. Women can never just relax and let things drift; they're always interfering, making lists, being a nuisance.'

'If they didn't, nothing would get done!' she argued firmly. 'All the traditions—Christmas and weddings, christenings and funerals—they have a symbolic importance; without them life slips away from us, the way topsoil blows away from a field if you have no hedges to mark it out. We have no sense of time passing if we don't notice the festivals of the year—the first cuckoo in spring, Midsummer night, bonfires at the winter solstice, the birth of a child, deaths in the older generation.'

'What has all that to do with a long engagement and a big white wedding?' Sam drily asked her.

'People remember occasions like that. You know what they say—that was the year the big elm blew down in the autumn storms...or that was the year Granny died just before Christmas...or the year Sam and Natalie got married. We need those markers in our heads and hearts. Nobody is so lonely as someone who has no home to go to at Christmas, nobody to share that day with, no present to give or receive. It shuts you out.

'One of my grandmother's sisters never married and

lived alone all her life. Every year we used to have her to stay at Christmas because she had nowhere else to go and my mother couldn't stand the idea of Aunt Lucy being alone on Christmas Day. Lucy was a boring old woman, she had a beard and she complained all the time. We never wanted her—but my mother insisted. Lucy was family. And my mother was right, you know. Family is important. So we can't just ignore what your mother wants, or my mother.'

Sam had been staring at her in apparent amazement while she talked. 'I've never heard you say so much before. You're serious, aren't you?'

'Yes, Sam. I understand why you want a quick, no-fuss wedding, but I know you love your mother and sisters—and they would all be very upset if we didn't have a proper, traditional wedding. They would feel cheated.'

'What about how we feel?' erupted Sam, scowling, and Natalie curved her hands around his face and looked into his eyes, smiling at him.

'We want to be together, don't we? And we have to do it the right way.'

Sam groaned again, in a very different way, his arms going round her, his hands exploring, caressing. 'Yes, and soon. The sooner the better—that's what I was saying. I want to wake up every morning and find you in my bed. We don't need all this fuss. All we need is each other. These traditional weddings take months to arrange.'

She couldn't deny it. Not when her mother was doing the arranging, with his mother on the sidelines, offering help and advice. Natalie knew life was going to be very fraught for them as soon as their mothers knew they were getting married. Sam had no real idea yet, even though he was so agitated. Natalie decided not to tell him, to let the real horror of it break on him slowly, hour by hour, day by day.

'We'll think of some fun things to do,' she promised, with a seductive under-her-lashes look.

'Witch,' Sam said, kissing her. 'I'm already thinking of them.' Then he gave her a hunted look. 'They'll try to make me wear morning dress—the full bit. Top hat, tails, pinstriped trousers! Well, I won't; you can tell them that. I am not walking down the aisle of some church in fancy dress. I want that clearly understood! Do you hear me, Natalie?'

'Yes, darling,' Natalie said fondly and with kind duplicity. 'I hear you.'

'And I'm not having a best man and long speeches.'

'No, darling.' Johnny would make a wonderful best man. Sam would come to realise that later, when he had had time to think and face the fact that he was going to have a best man, like it or not, because that was part of the ritual and their mothers wouldn't let him get out of it.

He thought, his mouth twisting. 'I suppose I have to buy you an engagement ring?'

She looked at him seductively again, amusement in her eyes. 'Unless you want me to wear your signet ring?'

'No, witch, I do not. That was what got me into this mess.'

She nodded serenely. 'You're probably right. But I think we ought to have one. I don't want anything ludicrously expensive—we'll save our money for more important things, like redecorating that house you want down by the harbour. But we can do most of the interior décor ourselves quite cheaply—lots of white paint and bright curtains and cushions cost very little but will look terrific. Our mothers will help me with sewing.'

Sam eyed her as if he was only now beginning to see

her clearly. 'You're a clever girl, aren't you? You can run my office, paint rooms, sew, make me very happy in bed—what else can you do? You aren't an amateur car mechanic as well, I suppose? No? Oh, well, never mind. I'm almost reconciled to having a white wedding. If that's the only way I'm going to get you, I'll put up with it. But you will keep me out of it as much as possible, won't you?'

'As long as you turn up on the day,' she promised. 'But you'll have to put up with a lot of so-called funny remarks when the people at work find out we're engaged, Sam.'

He looked morose. 'Do we have to tell them?'

'When I start wearing an engagement ring it's going to be difficult to keep it a secret! Grin and bear it, darling. But we'll tell our mothers before anyone else— they'd be very hurt if they weren't the first to know— and then we'll buy the ring and wait for the news to get round.'

'With my mother doing the gossiping it will be round the town within half an hour! The next week is obviously going to be hair-raising!'

He was all too accurate, but gradually the hilarity and teasing died down, and people began to accept them as a couple; they got invited together to parties thrown by other staff members, and everyone got used to seeing them having dinner together, or shopping at the weekends. The talk died down. They became part of the scenery.

All the same, the following months were pretty hectic. They each put their flats on the market and sold them; Sam's flat went first, so he moved in with his mother and they used the price of his flat to put down a deposit on an early Victorian house down by the harbour, with a breathtaking view of the sea from its balconied upper storey.

They had talked blithely about redecorating it themselves but were urged to have the roof professionally attended to—which was just as well because when the builders started work on it they found the roofbeams were riddled with dry rot, and they had to have new tiles, too. So the work took a couple of months and was only just finished by their wedding day.

Nevertheless they had begun cleaning and scrubbing floors and walls, stripping paint and wallpaper, before starting out on the new décor. They went to auction rooms and bought furniture at sales, at a lower price than new modern furniture; they had a new, modern kitchen built on to the back of the house, to replace the dark hole which had been laughingly called a kitchen in the agent's description of the house, and which they had stripped out and rebuilt as a utility room-cum-downstairs cloakroom. All of that had eaten into their shared capital, but they had both got a good price for their flats.

Natalie never had time to worry about the wedding day slowly advancing towards them. She had far too many other things on her mind. She and Sam still worked together every day, but in the evenings they went to their new home and worked on that, eating a quick meal first before painting and varnishing and doing the hundred and one jobs they still had to do.

She kept Sam out of most of the wedding discussions and work. It was Natalie and their mothers who wrote out all the invitations, ordered the food for the wedding reception, chose bridesmaids' dresses, flowers, a wedding cake, ordered wedding cars and buttonholes for the men.

Sometimes Natalie was exhausted when she finally got to bed. While Sam stayed with his mother Natalie had moved into the unfinished house down by the harbour, sleeping in one of the two spare bedrooms, which was immaculate now. It saved money and effort; she had less travelling to do. Quite often Sam stayed late at their future home, working with her, or cooked them both a meal while Natalie worked, and those were good evenings.

Stretching out in front of the log fire in their black Victorian iron grate, Sam said one night, yawning with weariness, 'I feel very married already. You were right about the decorating—it is fun! I just wish I didn't have to leave and drive all that way to my mother's house.'

He eyed her sideways hopefully, and she wrinkled her nose at him.

'We did agree that we wouldn't move in together until after the wedding.'

'We make love here,' he reasoned. 'Why can't I move in for good?'

They had discussed this many times before, but she patiently said, 'If you want to, Sam, okay. But I do feel it will make our wedding night that much more special if it is our first ever night together in our own home. That will be magic, won't it? It won't be the same if we're already living together. It will be the last barrier.'

'The final veil?' he teased. 'What terrible secret are you keeping from me? What will I discover once that veil drops and we start living together?'

That I love you more than life itself, she thought, but smiled in what she hoped was a mysterious way. They still had to discover so much about each other, and they were changing, acting on each other like chemicals mixed for the first time.

Did he realise how much he was changing? Today he had been up a stepladder, putting the final coat of white gloss paint on the hall walls, then he had stopped work to clean his hands with turpentine, washed, put on an apron and gone to get from the oven the lamb casserole he had put in a few hours earlier while she was varnishing the wooden stairs. He had laid the table, served their meal, called her to come and eat.

They rarely went out to dinner these days, rarely went dancing, or to a show in town. They preferred being alone, here, talking quietly, making plans when they weren't making love.

Sam was a different man now. That tense, driving look of impatience had gone. His eyes were contented and relaxed. He was happy, so was she—and she was going to make him happier.

'Wait and see!' she said, curling up at his feet and laying her head on his knee.

Sam lapsed into silence, stroking her hair. Ash softly drifted through the grate, the clock ticked, and Natalie daydreamed about their life together.

shocking pink

THEY WERE ONLY WATCHING...

The mysterious lovers the three girls spied on were engaged in a deadly sexual game no one else was supposed to know about. Especially not Andie and her friends whose curiosity had deepened into a dangerous obsession....

Now fifteen years later, Andie is being watched by someone who won't let her forget the unsolved murder of "Mrs. X" or the sudden disappearance of "Mr. X." And Andie doesn't know who her friends are....

WHAT THEY SAW WAS MURDER.

ERICA SPINDLER

Available in February 1998 at your favorite retail outlet.

The Brightest Stars in Women's Fiction.™

MIRA

Look us up on-line at: http://www.romance.net   MES415

Take 4 bestselling love stories FREE

Plus get a FREE surprise gift!

Special Limited-time Offer

Mail to Harlequin Reader Service®

3010 Walden Avenue
P.O. Box 1867
Buffalo, N.Y. 14240-1867

YES! Please send me 4 free Harlequin Presents® novels and my free surprise gift. Then send me 6 brand-new novels every month, which I will receive months before they appear in bookstores. Bill me at the low price of $3.12 each plus 25¢ delivery and applicable sales tax, if any*. That's the complete price and a savings of over 10% off the cover prices—quite a bargain! I understand that accepting the books and gift places me under no obligation ever to buy any books. I can always return a shipment and cancel at any time. Even if I never buy another book from Harlequin, the 4 free books and the surprise gift are mine to keep forever.

106 BPA CE65

Name	(PLEASE PRINT)	
Address	Apt. No.	
City	State	Zip

This offer is limited to one order per household and not valid to present Harlequin Presents® subscribers. *Terms and prices are subject to change without notice. Sales tax applicable in N.Y.

UPRES-696   ©1990 Harlequin Enterprises Limited